Cockroach Milk

Also by this author

Novels
Rebirth
The Rising
Drawing Dead
The Children of Hare Hill
The Naughty List

Gitmo Nation Novels
One Day in Gitmo Nation
A Gitmo Nation Christmas Carol
The Boy with Involuntary Social Network Disorder
Red Cell
Tales from Gitmo Nation

For Children, with Phil Ives
Krampus: A Christmas Tale

About the author

Scott McKenzie lives in Cheshire, UK with his wife and children. With no education in storytelling other than a healthy appetite for fiction in all forms, Scott simply thought he'd see if he could write a novel, and hasn't stopped since. Balancing family, work and a love of sport and movies, Scott writes his fast-paced stories in short sharp bursts.

ISBN 9798553645892

www.stardotfiction.com
Follow *.fiction on Twitter @StarDotFiction

www.scottamckenzie.com
Follow the author on Twitter @mckenz1e

Cockroach Milk was edited by Rebecca Hoffman. Read her blog, Rebecca's Red Pen, at rebeccamhoffman.blogspot.com

Cockroach Milk

A No Agenda Novel by

Scott McKenzie

Introduction

In the last few years, cockroach milk has emerged as a potential superfood, rich in nutrients and with significant benefits, both to the health of the consumer and to the environment.

Unfortunately, cockroach milk is very difficult to mass-produce. Any corporation that manages to solve the mass-production problem will corner the market and find themselves with a monopoly on the new superfood.

SM, November 2020

Prologue

Chapter 1

Lincoln, New Mexico
57 miles from Roswell

It was quitting time for the late shift at the cockroach milk factory. The siren sounded and the double doors opened, releasing the crowd of workers into the freezing midnight wind. Two of their number stopped outside the door: Wes and Alistair, or Al to his friends.

Wes' hands shook as he fumbled to open his brand new packet of cigarettes. The plastic wrapping blew out of his hands, into the pitch-black void that surrounded them. He looked up and saw the pathetic longing on Al's face. Wes sighed, emitting a cloud of steam from between his lips. It was too damn cold to go through the rigmarole of forcing Al to admit that he still hadn't bought his own cigarettes and wanted to bum another one off him. He'd lost count of the number of times that had happened this week.

"Take it," Wes said, handing a cigarette to Al.

"Thanks," Al said. "Got a light?"

Wes lit their smokes and they both sighed as they felt that initial hit of nicotine. Whatever it did to their bodies certainly wasn't good for them, but it sure as hell made them feel normal again after another shift in *there*. They shared a moment of quiet appreciation, staring out to the horizon, where the orange glow of the factory lighting blended into the darkness beyond.

A pair of bright headlights appeared in the distance. As they smoked Wes' cigarettes in silence, they tracked the movement of the headlights as they made their way closer. When they had got close enough to confirm that they belonged to a truck, they turned sharply up a road just past the entrance to the factory grounds.

"It's going up the hill," Al said.

"Third one I've seen this week," Wes said.

They watched as the truck made its way up the hill. When it came to a stop, its headlights illuminated the corner of another building at least as big as the one they worked in, maybe bigger.

"You ever wonder what goes on up there?" Al said.

"Every day I've worked here," Wes said, "but what can we do about it?"

Al thought for a moment, staring at the truck sitting next to the warehouse in the distance. "I don't know what it is," he said. "I just get a bad feeling about that place, like something's going on that they don't want anyone to know about. Hell, the place we work in is weird enough as it is. I figure if they're trying to keep secrets up there, then there's even weirder stuff going on."

"Why do you care?" Wes asked. "Just the other day you said you were close to quitting."

"It's just so weird here. I can't help myself. You've worked here longer than me; you ever know anyone who went in there?"

"Kinda. I knew a guy who knew a guy who had access."

Al didn't say a word. He didn't have to; his face said, *Well, what did he tell you?*

"I don't know what went on up there, Al. The guy I knew left a while back, but he gave me something before he left."

Wes looked around to make sure no one was looking their way, then dug in his jacket and produced a security pass attached to a lanyard. Al's eyes widened.

"Why did he give it to you?"

"He knew a guy who worked up there for one day. He said it freaked him the hell out, so he left. Moved away. Left his pass with the guy I knew, telling him to blow the whistle on what's going on up there if he ever got the chance."

"But he didn't do it?"

"Hell no. He didn't ask for it; didn't want it; gave it to me when he left; now I don't want it."

"So what are you going to do with it?"

"I tried not to think about it, just stuck it in my jacket. The guy's long gone. I bet it doesn't work anyway."

Al stared at the pass in Wes' shaking hand, then grabbed it—just to take a closer look, he told himself. It looked like a standard company pass: the green lettering of the company's name—Insectalat—ran along the top, followed by a photo of the ex-employee with his name and job title underneath. The pass had belonged to Jerry Morrison, Senior Facilities Technician, which meant he was a warehouse cleaner; someone who went under the radar, anonymous to management and warehouse staff alike.

"Don't recognise him," Al said, but didn't hand the pass back to Wes. He kept staring at it, feeling the weight of his own curiosity in his hand. "Can I keep it?"

Wes shrugged. "Sure. You'll be doing me a favour. But if anyone asks, I know nothing about it. Okay?"

Al nodded. "Okay."

A second pair of headlights appeared in the darkness; a second truck heading for the mysterious warehouse on the hill.

"Thanks for taking it off my hands, but I don't think it's a good idea to go up there. I bet there's nothing going on, and the only thing that'll happen is that you'll get yourself fired, and maybe blacklisted in this town."

Al didn't reply. He just watched the second truck as it made its way up the hill. Then he threw his cigarette to the ground and stamped it out with an air of determination that Wes hadn't seen in him before.

"You're probably right," he said. "But I just have to know. I'll tell you all about it tomorrow."

Then he gave Wes a wink and took his first step towards the warehouse on the hill.

Chapter 2

The trucks had been moved inside behind steel shutters by the time Al reached the top of the hill. With no visible signs of life, the warehouse felt deserted as he approached.

He was on a mission and welcomed the adrenaline-fuelled mix of fear, excitement, and anticipation that had been missing from his life since he had returned after serving his country. Now, even though his footsteps were leading him towards a warehouse in Lincoln, New Mexico, in spirit he was thousands of miles away, approaching a terrorist training camp in the desert.

Finding a door that had been left ajar, he positioned himself out of sight of anyone who might be standing behind it, then gently pushed it with his fingertips, trying to give the impression that it had been blown open by nothing more than the midnight breeze. The door let out a pained, rusty creak as it swung open. Al counted to five and, hearing no movement from inside, shot a glance through the doorway. There was no one there; nothing at all except a long grey corridor, lit from above by flickering strip lights.

Entrance secure, said the voice in his head. *Proceed inside.*

Al stepped over the threshold, moving with purpose along the length of the corridor. With no doors on either side, the only destination was a single solid metal door at the end of the corridor. A card reader hung on the wall next to the door, its bright red LED inviting Al to swipe the security pass Wes had given him. Al retrieved the pass from his pocket and stared at the face of the ex-employee.

No retreat, no surrender, he said to himself.

He held the security pass up to the reader. It gave a positive-sounding beep as the LED changed from red to green, followed by a loud clunk from inside the door frame. Hoping to stay out of the line of sight of anyone behind the door, he tried to push it open gently, but it wouldn't budge. Al realised he'd have to put his weight behind his effort to force it open. Thankfully, there was no one waiting to discover the trespassing factory worker. The door swung open to reveal another long corridor stretching out before him, dimly lit in comparison to the entrance, with the walls painted in dark tones. A staircase led upwards immediately to his right.

Al stepped inside and asked himself whether it would be best to close the door behind him to keep his infiltration a secret, or to leave it open in case he had to make a quick escape. The door itself gave him the answer, as it automatically closed and locked itself behind him. He tucked the security pass inside his pocket, making a mental note of exactly where it was in case he had to open the door with warehouse security chasing him.

Now Al had two options: proceed along the long corridor or take the staircase. If he'd been part of an armed squad with the mission to take control of the facility, he would always have been a member of the team that took the higher ground, waiting to ambush any aggressors from above. But he knew in his heart that he was just a lonely, curious guy checking out a creepy warehouse. If he had to get out of there quickly, it would be best to stay on the same level as the building's exit. He proceeded along the corridor.

At the end of the corridor, an opening to his right revealed a loading bay containing the two trucks that had grabbed his attention. They had been backed up against the opposite wall. With no one around, and confident that whatever tasks they had arrived to perform were now complete, Al ran across the loading bay, ducking into the thin gap between the two trucks.

He edged his way along, finding the rear doors of their trailers had been opened onto a ramp. At the top of the ramp was a wide opening where metal shutters had been pulled down, but not all the way. From where Al was standing, the gap under the shutters was directly in Al's line of sight. It was dark inside, and the light seeping in from the loading bay revealed only a few inches of a metal floor.

Al checked out the trucks and found them empty, apart from a stench hanging in the air so strong that it felt almost tangible. The putrid combination of body odour and urine made a single word pop into his mind.

Hobos.

Was that word a no-no these days? The older he got, the more he felt like he was losing track of the words he could and couldn't use. Whether the correct turn of phrase was "hobos," "the unhoused," or "people currently experiencing homelessness," he had a strong suspicion that these two trucks had, until very recently, been full of them. Looking back and forth between the empty trucks and the ramp leading up to the shutters, Al tried to put two and two together.

So, these two trucks full of hobos arrived, and someone opened them up and led the hobos up the ramp, closing the shutters behind them? Why?

Coming quickly to the conclusion that this warehouse did not have the air of a charitable homeless shelter, Al decided that whatever happened here was probably not in the best interests of whoever it had happened to. Al stared into the darkness beyond the shutters.

Proceed with caution, soldier. Watch your back.

Al made his way up the ramp and lifted the shutters just far enough to allow him to sneak underneath. Once inside, he paused for a moment, allowing his eyes to adjust to the darkness. The floor was constructed from a metal mesh, and he could feel a draught blowing upwards from below.

Al's first steps let out a loud clang that echoed downwards, so he did his best to tread as lightly as he could in his winter boots. He saw that he had to turn a corner up ahead, where dim red light seeped into the corridor from his unknown destination, a destination that was growing more ominous with every step. Still, there was silence all around him; no hint of the presence of the truck drivers or whoever—or *whate*ver—had been in the back of the trucks.

He was about to turn the corner when he trod on something soft. He lifted his boot and felt that it had stuck to the sole. It was big, almost as long and wide as his foot. He bent over and felt his way to the edge of the object. It was soft, and wet, and made a long, sticky sound like two pieces of meat being pulled apart as he removed it. Al struggled to examine the strange item in the low light. He edged towards the corner where the lighting was better.

For a second, it didn't feel real, then the realisation hit him that he had made a huge mistake by allowing his curiosity to get the better of him tonight. What he held in his hand was a human ear, attached to a strip of skin containing part of a bushy sideburn. He dropped it to the ground and nearly puked at the sound of the wet splat it made when it hit the metal floor. A squelch greeted him when he lifted his other boot, and he didn't bother checking what was stuck to it. Then he took a step round the corner, conscious that his curiosity was overriding the voice in his mind pleading with him to turn back and get the hell out of there.

The corridor opened out onto a large square hall. Bathed in red light from high above, the metal floor was covered in pieces of human bodies; some little more than shredded strips of meat, others were full body parts still wrapped in torn clothing.

Al looked up and saw a raised walkway encircling the hall. A beam of white light appeared from above, scanned the hall, then settled on him. He froze for a second, then every fibre of his being screamed at him.

Run!

As he turned towards the exit, he heard the fuzzy sound of voices talking over a radio.

"We still got one in here. Over."

"A survivor? Over."

"Negative. Unwanted visitor. Over."

Al focused on the shutters and ran as fast as he could, the clang of his boots on the metal floor announcing his exact position.

"Securing the facility. Over."

With those words, the shutters began to close. Already running at top speed, Al could do nothing but curse the dramatic decline in his athletic ability after he left the armed forces as he watched the shutters slam into the floor, extinguishing the light from the loading bay, and the hope it represented. Despite being certain that rattling the shutters and trying to open them with his hands would be nothing more than a futile exercise, he still did it anyway. His suspicion was proven correct, and now he was left feeling like the loneliest man in New Mexico.

Suddenly a voice boomed over a hidden speaker system. "Sir, please make your way into the main hall."

Al froze to the spot, unsure whether to comply or to stand his ground in some futile act of defiance. The voice immediately read his indecision.

"Sir, we don't have time to waste. Any delay will only serve to make this situation worse for you."

Al trudged back into the main hall, trying to step over the pieces of torn-apart human flesh, and failing on many occasions. He stopped in the centre of the hall, where four torch beams converged on him.

"You came here for a reason," the voice said. "What was it?"

"I want to know what goes on up here. There's something rotten in Lincoln, New Mexico."

"How very dramatic. Who else knows you're here?"

Al said nothing.

"Well?" the voice demanded, growing impatient.

Not wanting to get Wes into any trouble, he said, "No one knows I'm here. I'm on my own."

"I don't believe you, but like I said, I don't have time to waste on an interrogation, so we'll go straight to the execution."

The voice's throwaway words caught Al off guard. *Execution? Did he really just say the word "execution"?* He looked around, frantically searching for any kind of exit or help, but knowing that his situation was hopeless.

"Let's get this over with," the voice said. "Any final questions?"

Al scanned the pieces of flesh stuck to the floor all around him. "They were all hobos, weren't they?"

The voice laughed. "That's not very 'woke' of you. Yes, they were all people who were experiencing homelessness. Now they're people who are currently experiencing the afterlife."

Al opened his mouth, desperate to say something—anything—that would stand between him and whatever inevitability was quickly creeping up on him. But no words came.

"You came to see what goes on up here," the voice said, "and now you're going to see it."

The torch beams were extinguished. Al heard no footsteps. The men who had been watching him from above had decided to stay where they were, eager spectators of whatever was to come.

For a brief moment, the hall fell silent. Then Al heard a low rumbling sound coming from straight ahead. As it grew in volume, he felt the floor shake beneath his feet. Then an enormous bang rang out, the sound of a large object colliding with the metal wall across the hall from him. That was when he realised it wasn't a wall; it was a door. A clunk of machinery was followed by a thin line of bright red light spilling into the hall from the floor, which got taller and taller as the door began to rise upwards.

A strange, distorted shadow was cast across the floor, edging towards Al as the door crept higher. Within the rectangle of bright red light was the silhouette of a mass of moving parts that Al's brain struggled to process. The door was still rising when the writhing mass leapt for Al.

In his dying moments, he knew for certain what was really going on at Insectalat, and why the terrible truth had been kept secret.

Part 1: What Polly Did Next

Chapter 3

War in the Middle East was making me more money than I could spend. In a unique situation brought about by a combination of corporate bureaucracy and government corruption, the longer the war went on, the more commission I was paid every month. The government in question was that of the United States of America, led by our Republican President, Harold Franklin Green, and the company who paid me was Synergy Services, a multinational corporation that counted me as one of its newest and highest-flying account executives.

On my second day with the company, I had been the only person available to tag along for a meeting with Vice President John O'Grady at the White House. The sales lead had been brought about by nothing more than a call to the office that morning, with the message that the President had seen Synergy's TV commercial and wanted to discuss our corporate decision-making services. I was taken off my induction training and sent to the White House alongside Carl Dunning, an experienced account executive. But I was the one the Vice President took a shine to, giving us the opportunity to close a deal so huge that Synergy

Services went from being on the verge of laying off staff to exceeding sales targets and paying everyone a record bonus.

In my first week with the company, I had become a rock star. The board made an example of me in multiple ways. I was a new starter who had hit the ground running; I was a young woman who could do a deal with the wrinkly old white guys of Washington; in short, I was the future of the company. Several months on from what everyone at the Washington office referred to as "The Deal," the high-fives from strangers in the corridors had been replaced by passing quips from colleagues, asking where the next deal was coming from, like I was a stage magician preparing for a brand new show.

I could only smile and offer nothing more than "Wait and see" in reply, but in truth, I had nothing more up my sleeve. My boss told me I could choose any job within the company. In the most impressive piece of corporate lingo I had ever heard, he said the board's desire was to make me a "lighthouse employee for the art of the possible." Feeling overwhelmed with everything that had happened in such a short space of time, and hoping to stay under the radar, I requested the opportunity to complete my training and induction period with the company, the same as any other new employee. My plan backfired; the request to start at the bottom was held up by my superiors as yet another example of what a great role model I was.

And on top of all that, the money kept rolling in. Under the terms of "The Deal," I received one percent commission on the value of each transaction. The initial sum the government paid into the fund was one billion dollars, and they had already burned through more than half of it. The deal was based on Synergy providing the government with an outsourced decision-making service, with higher-risk outcomes costing the most and with an associated guaranteed pay out in the event of the decision in question leading to legal penalties. In basic terms, Synergy were providing insurance against bad decisions. With a President in the White House who previously had a pathological inability to make difficult decisions, the metaphorical floodgates opened. Even the President's assassination couldn't slow down the decision-making. If anything, the decision-making requests came through with greater frequency after his death.

As the war in the Middle East lurched from one catastrophe to the next, each month's pay slip reminded me of my role in making those decisions. My pay slip at the end of my first month with the company was a standard twelfth of my basic annual salary. But then my take-home pay in my second month was a six-figure amount, a *high* six-figure amount, even after taxes, student loan payments, and other assorted deductions. Pay slip number three contained a low seven-figure amount. Ever since, the monthly incoming transactions on my bank statement read like that of a lottery winner, but they were coming month after month. The feeling of punch-the-air instant wealth was tempered by daily reminders on every news channel of the destruction in the Middle East brought about by the administration's new-found ability to make very bad decisions very quickly.

On the other hand, Carl did not appear to be feeling that same pang of guilt that I did. The month before the first commission came through, he left his family, bought a penthouse apartment, and moved in with a stripper half his age called Raven. As soon as the deal—unofficially branded as "Conscience For Sale" by the Synergy sales force—became widely known in political circles, Synergy started receiving enquiries from governments all over the world, and Carl found himself being promoted to the position of Vice President of Global Public Decision Services, making him responsible for all Conscience For Sale deals to governments all over the world. Since Synergy Services operated worldwide with an impenetrably complex corporate structure, there was nothing to stand in the way of Carl's team selling their services to opposing nations of the same military conflict, without any legal obligation to divulge any conflict of interest. All of this coincided with a rise in reports of the development of chemical and nuclear weapons, a surge in the numbers of child soldiers representing allied forces in civil wars, and a renewed eagerness by third world governments to use mass executions as a way to curb civil disobedience.

After several months of trying and failing to lie low within the madness that had erupted at Synergy Services, I received a request from Vice President of Sales Carter Fox to pop into his office for a quick chat. He laid the situation out as he saw it: I had been instrumental in the deal that had reinvigorated the company, but whilst my partner in the deal was going from strength to strength, he got the impression I had been struggling to engage with the corporate culture.

After reflecting on this feedback for a moment, I said I agreed with his assessment and then encouraged the Vice President of Sales for Synergy Services to take my job and shove it up his warmongering ass. He chose to interpret those words as my notice of resignation with immediate effect.

Chapter 4

"How is your new job going?"

"It's going really well, Mom," I lied.

Sometimes I wished I could trade places with my mother. For the fifth time in less than twenty minutes, she had asked me the same question, and for the fifth time in less than twenty minutes, I had lied to her. There was nothing in her reaction to indicate that I had been repeating myself. Had we been anywhere else, a casual observer would have no suspicion about my mother's condition, but sitting here in the TV lounge at the Hillary R. Clinton Memorial Institute, I was acutely aware of the distance in her eyes.

I had begun to come to terms with the distance. My mother looked the same, had the same memories up to a point last year, but was somehow unable to create new memories. Sometimes we would sit here, reminiscing about my father, a soldier who had died in service when I was young. Those were the times when it was easy. But I found it hard when she wanted to talk to me about things that were happening when she fell ill. I had no option but to play along, knowing that I would be repeating the same act for the rest of my mother's life. No matter how much we talked about

21

the past, she always brought the conversation round to the present, with a dreaded, inevitable question.

"Have the doctors given you the results of my tests?" she asked.

"Yes," I said, happy to be telling her the truth, or at least a version of it.

"What did they say?"

I looked away, desperate not to catch the hope in her eyes. But every time I did that, she picked up on it and then asked the same question.

"Oh Polly, is it bad news?"

Just like countless times before, I nodded and recited my stock response, finding it harder and harder each time to make it sound like this was the first time I was breaking the news to her.

"The doctors say they have no definitive diagnosis for your condition. What they do know is that there's something wrong in your brain that means you can't make any new memories. They say the condition is degenerative, which means your long-term memory will start to erode, leaving you with fewer memories that will shrink further back into your youth the older you get."

This moment was bittersweet every time I came to visit. I saw the pain these words delivered, and the realisation as she scanned her surroundings that she wasn't at home in her own front room; she was in an institution with other people who also had visitors with similar looks of concern on their faces. But it was in this moment, when the penny dropped, that I had my mother back. In that fraction of a second, I could hear the words in her head.

What the hell am I doing here, surrounded by all these crazy old people?

Then, as she considered how to articulate her thoughts out loud, those thoughts disappeared, and she turned to me with that distance back in her eyes.

"Well, thanks for coming to see your old mother. I'm sure the doctors will have the results by the time you come back."

"If you want my opinion, it's down to those drugs you took when you stopped smoking."

I surprised myself with those words. It was the first time I had voiced that opinion. To me, there was an obvious link. My mother had smoked twenty a day for almost forty years, with only a brief, reluctant pause in the last few weeks before I was born. Then last year, her health insurance company gave her an ultimatum: quit smoking using their recommended smoking cessation aid or she would lose her coverage. Leaving her with no real choice at all, she accepted the offer of the free medication and, within six weeks, her memory started to fail. I had put the pieces together myself, concluding that the free medication, hastily supplied by the insurance company and with a rapidly approaching expiry date on the packet, was the reason for her sudden decline.

With grim predictability, the doctor appointed by the insurance company to assess my mother's condition did not come to the same conclusion. In his opinion—which was therefore the opinion of the insurance company—forty years of smoking with little physical exercise was much more likely to be the root cause of her condition. After all, he was seeing many patients just like my mother with similar symptoms.

The insurance company paid out just enough to provide home care for her, which amounted to little more than a couple of home visits a day from an overworked healthcare technician who was always already late for her next visit by the time she arrived.

When I hit the big time at Synergy, I used my first bonus to get my mother into one of the best care homes in the DC area, and then put a lump sum in trust to pay for her care indefinitely. My mother had no knowledge of this, no matter how many times I explained it to her. Her memory had been frozen in time by the drugs, which she started taking just before I started with Synergy.

I kissed and hugged her. "I'll come and see you again soon."

"Okay, sweetheart," she said, then settled back into her chair and locked onto the TV screen, which was tuned to a news report on the recent election of Frank Oates as President of the United States.

Chapter 5

Confident that I had been stood up, I thought it better to give up on yet another douchebag, rather than appear desperate by sending a "where are you?" message.

"You want another?" the barman asked, gesturing towards my empty bottle of Samuel Adams.

"Sure."

Just because some idiot couldn't be bothered to send a message apologising for being late, not being interested in me anymore, or being dead, I saw no reason to abandon the night just yet. The bar was pretty full and I was enjoying listening to the politically-themed lounge band playing in the corner, who called themselves the Wes Clark Seven. Only in DC.

My sudden wealth, and the personal freedom brought about by quitting my job and putting my mother in a care home, had taken away a lot of the excuses I'd made to myself for not having someone else in my life, so I'd turned to dating apps. Now, three weeks and six terrible or aborted dates later, I was coming to the conclusion that there was some mileage in the theory that all men were pricks, or maybe just that all the good ones were gay or taken.

The barman took my empty bottle away and replaced it with a fresh cold one. I was about to hand over the money when I heard a voice to my right.

"If you get another one of those, I'll pay for them both."

The barman looked at me, asking with a raise of his eyebrows if I was cool with it. I turned to look at the man next to me, giving him a three-second assessment. Six feet tall, in his thirties, no wedding ring, dressed in a suit with a loose tie and unbuttoned shirt. First impression: random guy on his way home from work; won't take offence if a beer doesn't lead to a night of wild passion.

I shrugged my acceptance and thanked him. The barman gave the man his beer. We clinked our bottles and said "cheers."

"I'm Polly."

"Andy," he said.

"Is this your thing?" I said.

"Is *what* my thing?"

"Stopping in at a bar on your way home from work to see if you can pick up a girl."

"No," he said, shaking his head with a smile, "you've got me all wrong."

"Well, thank you for the beer, Andy, but I'm waiting for someone and they should be here any minute."

"Steve Powell, thirty-one, works for a lobbying firm?" The sly look in his eyes said, *I know something you don't know.*

"If you're him, then you look nothing like your profile picture," I said, trying to steady my nerves as the sense that this stranger had an advantage crept over me. "I've got a good mind to sue you for false advertising."

"No, I'm not him. Well, not really."

"You're creeping me out. You've got five seconds to tell me what you want before I pour the rest of this beer over your head and walk out."

I gripped the bottle in my hand and began counting down.

"Five."

"I think they were right about you."

"Four. Who?"

"The people I work for."

"Three. Who do you work for?"

"A group of concerned citizens standing up to the evils in our society perpetrated by the likes of Synergy Services and their customers."

"Two. I don't work for them anymore. What do you want from me?"

"Cards on the table: we want your help and we want the money you made at Synergy."

"One."

I stared at the bottle in my hand, then looked at Andy. As far as I could tell, he genuinely didn't know whether I was about to pour the contents over his head or not. I took a swig of beer and put the bottle back down. "Okay," I said, "you've got through the qualifying round. Your prize is another two minutes of my time."

Andy opened his mouth to speak, but I stepped in before he could say a word.

"Answer my questions first, then you can tell me more."

"Okay."

"My date tonight was a setup, wasn't it?"

Andy nodded.

"So what, you set this up so you'd know where I'd be, then the rest of your plan is based on buying me a beer and then asking me for my money?"

"Pretty much," Andy said.

"Does this approach work?"

"It's worked before."

"Okay," I said, and looked at my watch. "Your two minutes starts now. Go."

"Thank you. My name is Andy MacKenzie. I work for the Washington Post, but that's just my day job. I'm a member of a growing group of concerned citizens."

"Concerned about what?"

"Globalisation, or, more specifically, the corruption and enslavement of the population that is being enacted under the banner of globalisation."

"You sound like a conspiracy theorist."

"You must know it's not just a theory, Polly. You've seen things in your time at Synergy."

"What makes you say that?"

"Why else would you quit so early into a job where you were pulling in a million a month?"

I thought for a moment. Being conscious not to confirm or deny Andy's speculation, I said, "You said you want my help and my money."

Andy nodded.

"Elaborate."

"Okay," he said, taking a breath. "The group that wants your help call themselves the Resistance."

"Like in France in the Second World War?"

"Right. We have people on the inside, and people who used to be part of the inner circle."

"What inner circle?"

"The global government."

"You're talking about the Unified Nations? I thought that was just a drinking club for politicians from all over the world, mostly old white men."

"In one way it is, but they don't just get together to drink. They are the driving force behind globalisation and the architects of key events that drive their agenda forward."

"Events like what?"

"The assassination of President Green."

Those words stopped me in my tracks. "Now you definitely sound like a conspiracy theorist."

"Think about it. You've been to the White House. You did a massive deal with the Vice President. Do you think he was such a solid, upstanding citizen that the very idea of murdering his boss to further his agenda was beyond the realms of possibility?"

I heard myself saying my thoughts out loud. "They did the deal because the President couldn't make a decision."

Andy leaned in. "What can you tell me about the deal?"

Chapter 6

I lay in bed awake all night. I had left my apartment wishing for little more than a pleasant evening with a random guy who wasn't a total douchebag. But the night had taken an unexpected turn very early on.

I knew the logical thing to do was to get up and leave the bar when Andy—if that was his real name—headed into conspiracy theory territory, maybe calling him a weirdo on the way out. Was there really a shadow world government, with nefarious plans to enslave humanity, seizing as much power and money as they could along the way? To what end? Predictably, Andy said he didn't know; apparently that was what the Resistance was trying to find out.

The question I couldn't shake from my mind was why *didn't* I get up and leave the bar, calling him a weirdo on the way out? Lying in bed staring at the digits of the alarm clock as they ticked towards tomorrow, my thoughts kept coming back to something I had watched on TV late one night. It was a documentary about David Icke, a British man who had once been a sports journalist but abandoned that life to preach his version of the "truth." Andy's words had felt very similar to Icke's.

I remembered watching the part of the documentary when Icke was on stage, telling his followers about how the global government changed their minds about having everyone chipped for surveillance when they realised more than ninety percent of the population would do it willingly in the form of smart phones. Icke was a crackpot, but a compelling one. His delivery led his audience on a journey, where a domino effect led them from one conclusion to the next, each one a greater leap of logic than the last. I had stayed with him right up to the point where he asserted, with complete authority and conviction, that the global government was headed by shape-shifting lizards from outer space.

That was the moment when he lost me. When I talked to friends about it, I was surprised to discover how many of them had also watched it, and how many of them had felt the same way as me. Right up to the point where he dropped the bomb about space lizards, everything he said sounded entirely plausible. What evidence did any of us have that the authorities *didn't* want to implant tracking chips in every citizen? As the years passed, did it feel like governments, advertisers, and any other number of groups with questionable motivations were taking less of an interest in our whereabouts and what we were doing, or more? The David Icke documentary came back to me every so often, and with Andy's words from last night dancing around my mind, this was definitely one of those times.

When my alarm clock read 5:30, I resigned myself to a night without sleep and dragged my body out of bed, made a coffee, and slumped down on the sofa under a blanket. I grabbed the remote and turned on the TV. CNN appeared, with the newsreader reporting on the security preparations for President Oates's inauguration in the new year. Recent attacks against Unified Nations troops in Jabronistan by the terrorist group Al-Qirmizi had prompted a full review of safety procedures for the event.

The familiar pang of conscience hit me at talk of war in the Middle East, and I resisted the usual urge to zap the TV off again. I sipped my coffee and allowed thoughts and words to make their way around my mind.

We want your help and we want the money you made at Synergy.

Our correspondent in the Middle East tells us that four soldiers—two American, two British—were killed when an improvised explosive device detonated under their vehicle.

Your government wants to implant a microchip under your skin.

Who do you work for?

A group of concerned citizens standing up to the evils in our society perpetrated by the likes of Synergy Services and their customers.

Unnamed sources told our correspondent that their vehicle had not been fully fitted out with armour due to budget cuts.

As far as the government is concerned, you are nothing more than a slave.

What if I say yes?

Washington Monument. Midnight. Tomorrow.

I jerked awake and sat up straight. Where the hell was I? What happened?

I was still on the sofa. My coffee cup was sitting on the table in front of me, steam no longer rising from its surface. CNN was still on the TV. The time in the corner of the screen told me it was nearly two in the afternoon.

Typical, I thought. *I struggle to sleep all night, then as soon as I get out of bed and sit down on the sofa, I get a full eight hours.*

I cursed myself for not being able to sleep like a normal human being; for not having a job to compel me to fill my day with activity; for not doing more to stop the war that the TV news wouldn't shut up about. Then I thought about the opportunity a stranger called Andy had presented me with.

Chapter 7

The surface of the reflecting pool had frozen over. The sky was clear and the bright light of the moon cast the long shadow of the Washington Monument across the frozen surface. It was just a few minutes to midnight, and I hoped Andy would be on time. After waking up on the sofa, I had become convinced that I needed to know more about what he had told me, but as the seconds ticked by in the deep cold of a DC night in November, I felt that need ebbing away and the draw of my sofa and a blanket becoming ever stronger.

The silence was broken by the sound of an approaching motorbike, which appeared by the monument and tore along the side of the reflecting pool, screeching to a stop next to me. The rider, dressed all in black, dismounted from his bike and took off his helmet.

"I didn't know whether you'd come," Andy said.

"Ditto," I said. "I hope to God we're not staying here. It's freezing."

Andy walked over to me, holding out his bike helmet.

"You don't want me to put that on."

He nodded.

"I've never been on a motorbike before."

"Don't worry, I'm careful," he said, "trust me."

"You just said 'don't worry' and 'trust me' in the same sentence. I'm far out of my comfort zone here and you're doing nothing to allay my fears."

"Come on," he said. "Jump on the back. It's not far."

"Where are we going?"

"What difference at this point does it make? It's somewhere indoors, warmer than here, and it's not far away."

"Why does no one in this town ever give anyone a straight answer?" I said, then grabbed the helmet out of his hands and put it on. He got onto the bike first, then I swung my leg over behind him.

As if he was reading my mind, he said, "You don't have to hold on to me. You can hold onto the bar on the back if you want."

Behind me was a small bar, just big enough for me to grip onto with two gloved hands. Then he gunned the engine and spun the bike in a one-eighty, leaving a semi-circle of scorched tyre tread below us. As we shot towards the Washington Monument, my hands involuntarily leapt from the bar to Andy's waist. My reserve and hesitation to hold onto this stranger went out the window as I clung on, fearing for my life as we blasted through the parkland surrounding the monument and onto Independence Avenue.

From that point on, I lost track of where we were. I closed my eyes and tightened my grip around

Andy's waist like he was the safety bar across my lap on a rollercoaster. Every second that passed, I prayed that we would arrive soon, and that we would get there in one piece. When Andy eventually stopped, he had to pull my hands apart from around his waist. My legs were shaking as I got down from the bike.

"You were hanging on pretty tight," he said.

"I guess I start getting clingy on the second date," I said as I took off his helmet. In my mind, I looked like a model on a TV commercial from my distant memory, where she takes off a bike helmet and shakes out her hair like the perfect vision of beauty. In reality, I'm certain I looked like someone who had somehow survived after being trapped in the rubble of a collapsed building for a week.

"So you enjoyed your first ride on a motorbike?"

I tried to think of some kind of response that would make me sound coy, but still cool. "Who am I kidding?" I said. "I'm never getting back on that or any other bike again. I don't care how secret this place is—I'm getting a cab back home."

Andy laughed and said that was fine with him.

"Where are we?" I said, surveying our surroundings. We were standing outside a forgotten warehouse, in what appeared to be a large abandoned industrial estate. I spotted streetlights all around, but none of them were turned on. Any signs hanging on buildings and fences that hadn't fallen down were faded and tattered.

"This is just a temporary meeting place," he said.

I followed Andy through a hole in the fence and down a path overgrown with weeds to what decades ago must have been the main entrance to a cornerstone of the American manufacturing industry. Now the doors were hanging off their hinges, with just enough of a gap between them for us to squeeze inside. Andy clicked on a pocket torch and the thin, bright beam led us into the entrance hall, where I could hear the drip-drip of leaking water and felt an uneven, decaying floor beneath my feet.

"I thought you said it would be warm when we got here?" I said as I rubbed my arms to get my circulation going.

"I said it was warm*er*. Didn't say it'd be warm."

"You son of a bitch."

"You'll get over it," he said. "Anyway, you might not have come with me if I'd told you about this place up front."

He led us into a room and found the light switch on the wall. I expected nothing to happen, but most of the fluorescent tubes overhead eventually buzzed into life. Many years ago, this room had been an office where ten to twenty administrative staff had beavered away five days a week to support the activity that took place in the warehouse. Now, almost all the desks were gone and the beige paintwork on the walls was tarnished with streaks of green, grey, and brown as leaking water and damp had taken hold.

Only one desk remained, which was home to a shiny desktop computer so modern that it looked like it didn't belong in there. Andy hit a key on the keyboard and the screen came to life. He pulled out the only chair in the room from under the desk, then tapped at the keyboard and clicked the mouse until a video messenger window appeared. Then he hit the call button and made for the door, leaving me staring at a screen where I was making a video call all by myself.

"Where are you going?" I blurted out.

"I'm not needed for this. I did my job—I got you here. The less I know, the better. Don't worry, I'll wait outside until you're done."

"Every time you tell me not to worry, it has the opposite effect."

Andy opened his mouth to say something, then thought better of it. The ring tone from the video call window stopped. "You're connected. You'll be fine. See you outside."

Andy left the office, leaving me alone, staring at a video call window. Before I had the chance to consider running after him, telling him I wasn't sure about this, a face appeared on the other end.

"Hello, Polly," the man said. "I'm glad you could make it."

Chapter 8

The face on the video call was familiar, but his name refused to pop into my mind. He immediately latched onto the look of confusion on my face.

"I'm sure this is a very strange situation for you, Polly," he began, "so please allow me to bring you up to speed. My name is Jonathan Bigelow—"

That's it! I thought, then cut him off. "Wait a minute, aren't you dead?"

He laughed. "Miss Benton, despite reports to the contrary, I am pleased to report that I'm fighting fit and one hundred percent definitely not dead."

My face flushed; I felt foolish at my outburst. "But…" was all I could say.

"I promise: all will be revealed. First of all, you're right; at least as far as the rest of the world thinks, I am dead. In my mind, I *was* dead. Following the Great American Shoe Throwing, my life was in ruins. My career was over, and my children and ex-wife wanted nothing to do with me. I was sitting at the Washington Monument, working up the courage to take my own life, when a man on a motorbike appeared and handed me a phone. The person on the other end made me an offer; the same kind of offer I'm going to make to you, which I'm sure Andy has already mentioned."

"He said you want my help and my money."

Jonathan smiled. "He is very direct, isn't he? Well, there's no getting away from it—that's exactly what we want. It's encouraging that you've come this far already, and your head must be filled with many questions."

I nodded.

"Let me explain," Jonathan said. "Now, I'm certain that Andy would have told you a little about our group. We call ourselves the Resistance. We are a group of concerned citizens from many corners of the world, doing our best to stand up to the onward march of globalisation in the guise of the Council of Unified Nations. I could spend many hours spelling out all of our concerns in minute detail, but the reason we have approached you—and I suspect the reason you have come this far—is because you share our concerns. We know this because of your actions up to the moment Andy sat down next to you at the bar. During your time at Synergy Services, you were party to conversations and decisions of which most people in this world are blissfully ignorant. They think the decision to go to war is based on solid foundation of reasonable facts. But we both know the truth, don't we?"

"I can't argue with anything you've said so far," I said, "but what can anyone realistically do about it?"

"We are discovering that as we go. Certainly we do not expect a full dissolution of the Council of Unified Nations or a full abandonment of their plans any time soon, but the basic laws of physics tell us that a body in motion will continue indefinitely unless it meets with friction. Polly, we are that friction, and the bigger we become, the more friction we find ourselves able to apply to the force of the Council of Unified Nations."

"I'm still listening. I get it—you need my help. Now tell me why you need my money."

"You're a straight talker, Polly, and I respect that. I'll give you a straight answer: we need the funding. We have sponsorship from a number of wealthy individuals, but as we expand, our need for operating cash increases. Our ability to operate and protect the members of our group is directly dependent on the liquidity of our accounts. But I'll be honest with you: there is a second reason. We ask all members to make a personal contribution to the cause. This separates the talkers from the doers, the interested parties from the genuinely concerned citizens who are willing to commit to the cause. It doesn't matter how rich or poor you are, or what your background is, we expect all new members to contribute their fair share."

"Which is what?"

"Ninety percent of your immediately available wealth."

"Ninety percent of the money I have in the bank?"

Jonathan nodded. "And ninety percent of future dividends, say for bonus payments you may still be owed by a previous employer."

We both knew that was a hint that he knew a lot more about me than he was letting on, but I did my best to not let it break my stride.

"Regardless of how rich or poor you may be, ninety percent is life-changing. I'd probably be back to finding it difficult to pay rent in this town or buy groceries."

"No, no, you wouldn't have to worry about things like that. We look after our members, which means the Resistance would pay your rent if you chose to operate in an undercover or insider role, and if you choose to leave your current life behind, we would house you in one of our facilities, along with our other full-time operatives. You can make the decision about how you want to contribute towards our effort. Of course, you do have the option of leaving tonight and forgetting everything we talked about. In that scenario, all I would ask is that you keep our conversation secret, along with your knowledge of my continued existence."

I said nothing. The words "leave your current life behind" ticked over in my head. I thought of my mother, sitting alone with little clue where she was or why she needed people to care for her.

"I know your personal situation," Jonathan continued, "I know all about your mother's health problems, and I therefore assume that leaving your current life is something you wouldn't want to consider. Is that right?"

I nodded.

"Okay, so I'm going to make the choice easier for you. Join us, and you keep your current identity. We would move you to a new property of our choosing and then assign you a role as an insider at an organisation in which we have a particular interest. There, you would operate as a regular employee and await instruction from a member of the Resistance. That instruction might come within a day, or a week, or a year. It all depends on when we find a need to investigate the goings-on at your organisation."

"So I'll be on their payroll?"

"Of course. You would be required to donate ninety percent of your take-home pay to our effort, but to everyone else around, you would be just another employee."

I said nothing, trying to allow my brain to process everything.

"Now, you still have the option to decline my offer, but I need you to make a decision tonight."

"Tonight?"

"I'm afraid so. I don't like to leave things like this hanging—we've been burned in the past. I will stay on this call for as long as you need and answer any questions you may have, but I do not want to close the call until you give me a definitive yes or no."

"This is a lot to take in," I said. "It's a big decision."

"I don't think it is," Jonathan said, taking me by surprise. The look on my face must have given my feelings away. He carried on talking. "Right now, you are wealthy enough to support your mother, but now that you are no longer working, you have no purpose in life. Sure, you fill your days, but I don't think you want to face a future where more bad things happen around you and you are powerless to do anything about it. I am certain you feel shame and regret at your actions during your time at Synergy Services, and the decisions the government took as a result of those actions. Any sensible, right-minded person in your position would feel exactly the same. But your reaction to that situation leads me to believe you want to change things. I am giving you the chance to change things, and I'm the only person who ever will. In my mind, there is only one way forward for you, but you have to come to terms with it. What do you say?"

I stared at Jonathan Bigelow, the man on the other end of the video call who had faked his own death, forfeiting any chance of reconciling with his family. In my own way, I began to come to terms with the decision I had to make.

Chapter 9

Within ten minutes, I had accepted his offer. Now, sitting in a coffee shop surrounded by people going about their regular lives, I became acutely aware that I had thought of nothing else for the last two days since I had left the abandoned warehouse.

Andy had given me a lift back into the city—going slowly under the threat of me screaming in his ear the whole way—and I called a cab to take me home. Andy said we would probably see each other again, but he couldn't say when. Jonathan's parting words to me were to say that I should go back to my normal life and wait for someone from the Resistance to find me and deliver the details of my assignment.

I took a sip of my coffee and watched the people around me as they came and went. How many of them had the same concerns about society and the government as me? Probably most of them, but I was certain each one of them would measure themselves on a sliding scale that ran from "passing interest in current affairs" to "fully engaged but powerless to do anything about it." What excited me most about the offer from Jonathan Bigelow and the Resistance was that it gave me the ability to break through that scale, putting me in the category of people who could "do something about it."

My thoughts were violently torn from me as a man dressed in a bicycle courier outfit sat down in the opposite chair, uninvited.

"Polly Benton?" he barked at me.

"Erm, yes, hello?" I said, readying myself to protest at this invasion of my daydream when the penny dropped. "Are you—"

"Yes, that's right," he interrupted, shooting a look at me that told me not to be so stupid as to say the name of our secret organisation out loud in a coffee shop. "I've got something for you."

He opened up his backpack and pulled out a manilla folder, which was one of many in there. He handed it to me, but wouldn't loosen his grip on it.

"Don't do anything silly like reading this here," he said. "Okay?"

"Of course," I said, hoping the fact that I would have done just that was not obvious from the cool expression I was trying to project.

"Good," he said, letting go of the folder. "Everything you need is in there."

With those parting words he was gone, the third member of the Resistance to exit the stage of my life almost as quickly as he had stepped onto it. I looked again at the people in the coffee shop. Was anyone in here part of the Resistance too? Maybe more than one? How would I know? How would they know about each other? Without direct communication and coordination from the leadership, there's no way they would have known about each other, and I guess that was the whole point. I, like the others, was hiding in plain sight.

I finished my coffee and got up to leave, tucking the folder under my arm. Its weight felt far greater than the sheets of paper tucked inside.

The moment I shut my apartment door behind me, I threw the folder down and opened it up with a level of excitement and anticipation I hadn't felt since the last time I had to wait for exam results. The first page contained only three words:

Destroy after reading.

Turning that over, the second page contained only slightly more information. It read,

Your new address is:

Apartment 3A
The Keeper Building
Mellancon Boulevard
White Oak MD

So, I'm moving to White Oak, I thought, racking my brains for which major company or government department was based there. Page three read:

Turn over for details of your assignment.

Send a weekly report of your findings and progress to the following address unless told otherwise. Your report should be no longer than a single page and be sent via standard US post.

Box 339
El Cerrito CA
94530

If you need immediate help for any reason at any time, call 333-5510.
Memorise this number—it could save your life.

Page four was a letter, addressed to me at my new address, on letterhead from the Food and Drug Administration.

Dear Polly Benton,

Thank you for your application for the position of Trainee Inspector.

After careful consideration, I am pleased to inform you that we would like to offer you the position on a permanent basis, with your employment beginning on Monday, January 6th. At 9am on that day, please report to the main reception at the address listed at the top of this letter to begin your induction training.

The White Oak office will be your base location, but this is a mobile role and, as such, you should expect to travel all over the United States, sometimes at short notice. Therefore, you will

So, they've stuck me in the FDA as an inspector, I thought. If the Resistance wanted someone to travel all over the United States and be their eyes and ears within the government and private corporations, an inspector for the FDA felt like one of the perfect jobs to do just that.

The thought of spending a lot of time on the road troubled me when I read the letter but, upon reflection, I thought it wasn't too different from the job I had accepted with Synergy Services. They had me primed to travel all over the country to negotiate deals on their behalf, so I hoped the job of travelling inspector would be similar: onsite somewhere for a couple of days, then the rest of the week back at the office to write up and process the admin. That would still give me the opportunity to spend quality time with my mother, and maybe even build a life for myself,

while still fulfilling my obligations to my "real"
employer.

Simple as that, right?

Part 2: Monday 20th January

Chapter 10

The FDA referred to my first two weeks as my induction but, just like my induction at Synergy Services, it was a good old-fashioned corporate brainwashing. So old-fashioned, in fact, that I was left wondering whether any of the training material had ever been updated since the introduction of the Food and Drugs Act in 1906. Apparently, some of the benefits of my new vocation were:

1. A big initial salary with fine prospects for promotion; liberal expenses while travelling.
2. Exceptional opportunities for extensive travelling.
3. Frequent and intimate contact, both professional and social, with successful men of recognized standing in the commercial, scientific, and legal spheres particularly, such as presidents and other officers of corporations, leading manufacturers, U.S. District Attorneys, judges, noted scientific experts, etc.

Frequent and intimate contact with successful men. How lovely! Despite the lack of political correctness on show, over the two weeks of my induction I came to terms with the prospect of working for the FDA.

Point number two was the most accurate of the three: every inspector was expected to spend a significant amount of time on the road. It was no surprise to find that I was the oldest person in the room, surrounded by trainees fresh out of college, neck-deep in student debt and with no ties holding them down. The only exception was our trainer, a pleasant man in his late fifties who regaled us with stories from his thirty-plus years of paying his dues as an inspector.

By the end, every member of the class was eager to get their first assignment, myself included. My association with the Resistance simmered in the back of my mind, occasionally bursting forward to remind me why I was really there, but I came to realise that life in the FDA was something I could have been comfortable with even if I had signed up voluntarily.

Day one of week three was day one in the real job. It was like rebooting my time with the FDA all over again. With my laptop bag over my shoulder, I reported to reception at nine o'clock, where the man behind the desk made up a security pass for me. With well-rehearsed precision, he took my picture, then printed it onto a plastic card above my name, slipped it into a plastic sleeve, and attached it to a lanyard with the words "Food and Drug Administration" printed in an infinite loop. I felt a small pang of pride as I hung it around my neck.

He tapped at his keyboard, then said, "You're in hot desk zone six, on the third floor. Take the elevator, then go through the door to your right when you get out. Then find a desk and make yourself comfortable. A senior inspector will come and find you."

I followed his instructions and entered a room that felt the same as my old office at Synergy Services. About half the desks were occupied by men and women in suits hunched over laptops, transcribing notes from notebooks and piles of paper. It became clear to me at this moment that life on the road as an inspector for the FDA would be very similar to life on the road as a salesperson for a services company: long spells of unstructured activity outside the office, with occasional bursts of frantic paperwork upon your return.

I found a desk and set my laptop bag down on a chair—the internationally understood method for reserving a hot desk—then turned my attention to the search for a cup of coffee. I went back out to the elevators and found a door that led through to a kitchen area, where a line of suits was waiting at a coffee machine, eager for the first caffeine injection of the week. I grabbed a cup from the cupboard and joined the line. Everyone was standing in silence, their attention taken by a TV hanging on the wall showing a CNN report.

The newsreader said, "We now go to our reporter, Gravel Foden, who is on the scene. What are you learning, Gravel?"

CNN cut to Gravel, who looked like a quarterback turned news reporter, standing in front of a factory. "I'm here at the factory of Insectalat, the biggest employer in the town of Lincoln, New Mexico. If you haven't heard of Insectalat, then let me tell you that the company is leading the way in the production of insect-based foodstuffs, including bug burgers and their wildly popular cockroach milk, which has been billed by many industry experts as this year's new superfood due to the high levels of amino acids and other nutrients. What sets Insectalat apart is the fact that they've found a way to mass produce cockroach milk on an industrial scale, while all their competitors continue to struggle. Security and secrecy are paramount here at the factory, so it's no surprise that details surrounding the disappearance of one of their workers are sketchy. What we know so far is that one of the factory workers, who has been unofficially named by locals as war veteran Alistair Cameron, went missing two nights ago. He was last seen leaving the factory after his night shift. Insectalat representatives are saying there is no story here; they say he quit and hasn't spoken to anyone since, but I've spoken to people in the town who say Mr. Cameron's disappearance isn't the first of its kind. We've had official word from the FDA that they will be sending an inspection team here this week, so I don't think this will be the end of the matter as far as Insectalat is concerned."

The reporter's final comment brought murmurs from the men and women in front of me in the line for the coffee machine.

"I wonder who's getting that detail?"

"Have you ever tried cockroach milk?"

"A friend of mine tried it and said she'd never go back to cow's milk."

I reached the front of the line and made my cup of coffee. As I turned to make my way back to my desk, I found a pair of eyes staring down at me. They belonged to a tall man in his late forties. Not the type of late forties where the battle with beer and fast food has been fought and lost a long time ago; this was a man in his late forties who had the figure of someone who ate well and regularly visited the gym. I saw no happiness on his face, then remembered that this was Monday morning; no one had happiness on their face. I saw his eyes dart down to my security pass, then back up to my face.

"You're Polly Benton," he said. It was a statement, not a question. "You're new."

"Pleased to meet you," I said, holding out a hand. "This is my first day in the office."

After a pause so long I thought he might leave me hanging, he eventually shook my hand.

"Bill MacGregor," he said. "Don't get too comfortable in the office, though."

"Why?"

"We've been given an assignment."

I was pleased it took less than a second for the penny to drop. "I'm your partner?"

"That's right."

"What's our assignment?"

Bill waved a thumb over his shoulder at the TV on the wall. "That report you were just watching."

"The cockroach milk factory?" I said, hearing a gasp from across the kitchen.

Bill nodded. "Finish your coffee, then go back home and pack an overnight bag. We're going to New Mexico."

Chapter 11

I got in and out of my apartment within twenty minutes. Packing for New Mexico took five minutes; I spent the rest of the time poring over the first communication to my true employer.

Before that day, I had paid more attention to writing letters by hand to only one person: Santa Claus. I grabbed a few sheets of paper from my printer and dug a pen out of a drawer, then sat down at my kitchen table and, with a bit of trial and error, carved out a note in handwriting that I didn't recognise.

To whom it may concern,

I am about to get on a plane to Lincoln, NM, to visit the Insectalat factory where one of the workers has gone missing. It was reported on CNN this morning. My partner is a man named Bill MacGregor, who has worked for the FDA for a long time.

I'm on the 14:45 flight from Dulles to Roswell. I'll write again if I make any significant discoveries.

Kind regards,

I stuffed the letter into an envelope and addressed it as I had been directed in the folder the courier had given me. Then I left my apartment, dropped the letter into a post box, and stopped in to see my mother on the way to the airport. I greeted her with a hug and standard "hello," learning from the mistake I'd made earlier in the month when I'd wished her a happy new year and then spent a full hour trying to explain that no, it wasn't just New Year's Day a few months ago.

We sat down in the TV room and my mother opened with one of her usual questions.

"How's the new job going?"

Even though the new job I was now telling her about wasn't the new job she had in her mind, my conscience was a bit clearer about the direction in which I took the conversation.

"That's why I've come to see you," I said. "I'm going away for a few days, so I wanted to see you before I leave."

"Where are you going?"

"New Mexico." I stopped short of giving her the gruesome details of my destination.

"Now that you work for a big corporation, I suppose they'll be putting you on the company jet."

There it was—the quick reminder that my little white lies were just a load of baloney.

"Something like that," I said, swerving around the emotional obstacle she had thrown in my way. "In fact, I'm on my way to the airport right now."

"Well, don't let me stop you," my mother said as she got to her feet.

"It's okay, really," I protested. "Sit down, I've got plenty of time to get to the airport."

"No, no, no," she said, taking my hand and trying to pull me to my feet. "You need to go now. You never know what might happen between here and there. As my mother used to say: 'there's many a slip 'twixt cup and lip.'"

I had a flashback to her trying to get me out the door to school, fearing I'd be late, but every day I got there to discover I was the first kid in the playground. There would be no arguing with her. Once that bomb had been dropped, all resistance was futile. Long ago, I made a promise to myself that if I had children, I would never pass that stupid phrase on to them. If it ever passed their lips, it would not be preceded by the words 'as my mother used to say.'

"Okay," I sighed as I stood up, exactly as I had on a daily basis more than twenty years ago, "I'll go, but I'll come to see you as soon as I get back and we can spend a bit more time together."

"Perfect," she said. "Now you go straight to the airport and I'll look forward to hearing about all the excitement of your trip when you get back."

Chapter 12

Bill barked the name of a motel at the cab driver, then we didn't say another word to each other for over an hour until we got there. I sat back and watched the sun set over New Mexico as we travelled from Roswell airport to Lincoln.

After almost eighty years, businesses in Roswell, New Mexico were still trading on the strange events that brought notoriety to the town and made it the centre of the universe of conspiracy theories about alien species making contact with us. It seemed to be a mandatory requirement for every sign and shopfront to be emblazoned with pictures of little green men, and for the lettering to be heavily inspired by sci-fi movies and TV shows. The alien theme gradually dissolved the further we got from Roswell, until the view out of my window could have been peaceful farmland anywhere in America.

Bill managed to get us checked in to the motel without saying a single word to me. The only hint I got that he was prepared to acknowledge my existence was when he slid one of the two room keys across the motel reception desk to me, and grunted the words, "Meet down here at nine a.m." Then he left the reception area, almost breaking into a sprint in an effort not to have to walk with me.

"Enjoy your stay," the man behind the reception desk said.

I thanked him and went outside to see Bill ascending the stairs two at a time. I checked my key and noted that my room was on the ground floor. *Did he call ahead to make sure we weren't in rooms next to each other?* I thought. I cast any dark thoughts from my mind, certain in the knowledge that I hadn't known Bill long enough to piss him off. *People are weird*, I thought. *And you tend to find out just how weird they are when you travel with them.*

I found my room and stepped inside. It was the barest, most tired-looking room I'd ever stayed in. The stale smell of dust and sweaty human traffic hung in the air. There was a double bed on one side of the room and a TV on the other; an old CRT sitting on a stand with all the cheapest possible components plugged into it to make it work. I set my bag down on the faded patterned bed sheets and wondered how many people had slept beneath them since the last time they had been washed. The door at the end of the room was ajar, the thin gap hinting at the bathroom within, but I didn't feel ready to venture in there just yet.

Checking my watch, I realised I was facing the prospect of a whole night alone in this awful room, so I turned and left, locking the door behind me. The road was lined with auto repair workshops and office blocks with "To Let" signs hanging outside, but there was one beacon of light that gave me hope. Across the road from the motel was a bar advertising beer, food, and sports on giant TVs.

Inside, the bar was warm and busy, with a welcoming atmosphere of people laughing and cheering at the TVs dotted all over. Tonight, they were showing a college basketball game between two local sides, the Lobos and the Mustangs. I fought my way through the crowd to order a beer and a burger.

"Are you new here or passing through?" the bartender asked me as he poured my beer.

"Passing through," I said.

"Right. So you don't work with the rest of these guys?"

I took another look at the crowd around me. "Everyone here works together?"

The bartender nodded. "Up at the bug milk place."

"Insectalat," I said.

He brought my beer over. "You've heard of it, then. No surprise, I guess, since it's been all over the news this week."

"Did you know the man who went missing?"

"As much as I know anyone else in here. They all come in at the end of their shift, or most of them do anyway, which is good for me because I hear they pay well up there. These guys are from the day shift. If you're still here just after midnight, you'll see the late shift roll up too."

"Have you ever worked up there?"

The bartender smiled. "So I got a newcomer sitting at my bar, says she's just passing through, and she's asking me questions about the bug milk factory where one of the workers has gone missing. You're what, FBI, CDC?"

"FDA."

The bartender shrugged. "All the same alphabet soup to me, sweetheart, but do you want some advice?"

"Sure."

"Keep the questions to yourself. For tonight, at least. Is there anything weird going on up there at the factory? Maybe. You work behind this bar long enough, you'll hear some stories, I can tell you. Most of it BS, I don't doubt, but what I do know is that they pay well, and the people who work there like getting paid well, and I also like the fact that they get paid well. Now, you're here to do a job and I get that, but if you wanna sit there and drink your beer and eat your burger in peace, you'll do yourself a favour and hold off talking shop 'til you're on the clock. Know what I mean?"

"Understood," I said. "Thanks for the advice."

I left my spot at the bar and found a table in a corner where I could pass the time watching the people in the bar watching the game. I love people-watching. Airports are the best, where you get one of the most complete cross-sections of society, but bars are pretty good, too. The only problem for a woman on her own is the unwanted attention it brings, but the male-heavy clientele of the bar had their attention taken by the game on the TV. My observations matched what the bartender had told me: by the way they talked to the bartender and each other, all the people in here seemed to be regulars. They had plenty of money on them to buy beers and bar food, and this was a Monday night, not a weekend blow-out.

My burger arrived, which I washed down with a few more beers as the evening wore on, until the point when I started to feel like I really should retire to my uninviting bed across the road. I decided to answer the call of nature in the bar, figuring that the female bathroom in a male-heavy bar had a chance of being cleaner than the one in my motel room.

I was washing my hands at the washbasin when something on the floor caught my attention. My eyes detected movement, and I looked down to feel immediate revulsion at the discovery of a cockroach scuttling around my feet. I reeled backwards, a shiver shooting down my spine. This cockroach was about an inch or so long—tiny compared to some specimens we had been told about in the induction training—and I knew I would have to get used to being around them if I planned to be working for the FDA for any decent period of time.

I was about to turn and run from the bathroom when a second cockroach appeared. But this was no ordinary cockroach; this one froze me to the spot in disbelief, in genuine fear at what it might be about to do. If the first cockroach had been the baby bear, this second one was undoubtedly the daddy. It must have been six inches long and two inches wide. Where the baby had moved in silence along the tiled floor of the bathroom, the daddy made an unnatural clicking as it zipped from its hiding place. The baby cockroach seemed to turn away from it, but the daddy pinned the baby down, which was followed by a loud crunch. I stood in shocked silence until I realised the daddy cockroach was eating the baby.

I let out an involuntary shriek and stepped backwards. The daddy stopped and turned its antennae in my direction. I turned and ran, slamming the bathroom door behind me, checking that there was no gap beneath the door for the cockroach to squeeze through. There was a gap, but it was only big enough for a small sliver of light to spill into the corridor from within the bathroom.

I took a moment to compose myself, to come to terms with the horror of what I had witnessed, when I heard a sound from the other side of the door. It was a combination of light scratching and bumping, a common occurrence for cat owners as their pets try to get through a locked door. But I knew there was no cat inside the bathroom. A shadow in the light under the door, a couple of inches wide, was moving frantically left and right.

It's trying to get through the door, I thought. *It wants to break through the door to get to me!*

Thirty seconds later, I shut the door to my motel room and locked it behind me. I sat on the bed, holding my head in my hands, trying to compose myself. My heart was pumping hard in my chest. I felt faint.

What the hell just happened?

I had never heard of cockroaches growing to the size of the beast I'd just seen; the beast that had just attacked me. It had killed the smaller cockroach—was that normal behaviour in nature? It struck me that nothing about tonight's encounter was natural. My thoughts turned to the reason I was in Lincoln, New Mexico.

How was that massive cockroach related to the Insectalat factory? Did it escape? It felt unlikely that the two things weren't related.

I got into bed with a determination to recommend the bar across the road for inspection, right after I'd found out what was going on at the Insectalat factory.

I didn't sleep well.

Part 3: Tuesday 21ˢᵗ January

Chapter 13

In the morning, I opened my door to find Bill waiting outside.

"Good morning," he said. "How did you sleep?"

"Fine," I lied.

"Our taxi will be here soon. Sorry I went straight to my room last night. I had a few calls to make. Did you get out at all?"

"I went to that bar across the road," I said, pleasantly surprised at Bill's congeniality this morning.

"Any good?"

"The food was okay," I said, "but I'll be making a recommendation to have it inspected."

"Really? What did you see?"

"A cockroach in the bathroom."

"Maybe we'll take a look over there tonight. Was it just the one?"

"Actually, no. I saw two: a small one and a monster."

"A monster? How big?"

I showed him the approximate size with my hands, like a fisherman boasting to his friends about his enormous catch at the weekend.

"Wow," Bill said, "that must have been a beauty."

Our conversation was brought to a halt as the taxi arrived. The journey only took a few minutes. The Insectalat plant was just outside the main built-up area of Lincoln, which fuelled my suspicion that its close proximity had something to do with the homicidal cockroach from last night. On our approach, I spotted what looked to be two main buildings: a warehouse emblazoned with the Insectalat logo, surrounded by a busy parking lot, and another warehouse of a similar size on the hill, a short distance behind the main warehouse. I saw no buzz of activity around that building.

The taxi pulled up outside the first building, where a forty-something man in a suit was waiting for us. He introduced himself as Jason Campbell, the site manager. He gave Bill the bone-crunching handshake that men in suits tend to share, but the handshake he offered me was like being greeted by a piece of wet lettuce. Did Jason and Bill already know each other well, or was Jason just another one of those businessmen who think they might break this pretty little lady's hand with their oh-so-manly handshake?

"So happy to have the FDA here," Jason said through gritted teeth. "We're happy to help any way we can, and answer any questions you may have."

"First question, Jason," Bill said.

"Go ahead."

"Where can we get a cup of coffee?"

Jason laughed, and told us to follow him inside. He took us to the reception desk, where we went through the process of signing the visitor's book and being issued visitor's passes, a process I would have to get used to in my life as an FDA inspector. We were then escorted along a corridor to a break room. Jason poured the coffee and handed the cups to us.

"Milk?"

I was on the verge of saying "Yes, please," but Bill spoke first.

"What kind of milk is it?" he asked.

"Our own house blend," Jason said with a grin He went to fridge and returned with a carton of cockroach milk. From a distance, it looked the same as any other milk carton: tall, white, and dotted with pleasant colours and a few positive words here and there. I'd seen the carton on the shelf in the grocery store before, but I'd never really paid it any attention, choosing to slide past it as quickly as I could, with precisely zero intention of ever picking it up.

I took the carton from Jason and examined it. "Insectalat Milk" was printed in large letters on all sides. At first, I found no mention of the word "cockroach," but soon found it in small print on the back. I handed it back to Jason.

"I'll pass," I said. "I like my coffee black."

"Shame," he said, then turned to Bill. "What about you?"

"Sure, I'll take it," Bill said with surprising gusto. He poured the milk into his coffee and stirred it. I watched him take a sip, as if I was expecting him to start coughing or choking, but all he did was turn to me and say, "You've never tried it, Polly?"

I shook my head. "Never."

"Well, we need to rectify that right now," Bill said. He pulled an empty mug out of the cupboard, poured a small measure of cockroach milk into it, and handed it to me. "Here, try it."

I hesitated. I knew that this wouldn't kill me, but the situation felt weird. Bill and Jason's eyes were on me, the new girl. I hadn't felt peer pressure like this since being labelled uncool by all my so-called friends at high school for choosing not to vape along with the rest of them.

"Go on, try it," Jason said. "How can two million—and counting—Americans be wrong?"

I looked into the mug. Against the white porcelain, the milk had a light blue tinge, which immediately brought to mind Luke Skywalker's blue milk from Star Wars. Sensing no socially acceptable alternative, I lifted the mug, breathed in the aroma, and took a tiny sip.

"Yeah!" Jason cheered, and gave me a short round of applause. "Well, what did you think?"

"It's actually not that bad," I said honestly.

"Remind me never to offer you a job in Marketing," Jason said with a laugh.

I took another sip, this time a bigger one, and I was happy to do so. "It tastes like regular milk, only sweeter," I said.

"That's right," Jason said. "We like to think our milk is like a powered-up version of cow's milk.

Everything is bigger and better. It's very high in protein and calories, and the energy is released slowly, which gives our customers high energy levels all day long. Scientific studies have shown that it helps to alleviate pain and repair damaged muscle and skin tissue, so it's no surprise that long distance runners are some of our best customers. But above all, it tastes great and I'm pleased that's the first thing you noticed."

"It's kind of a funky blue colour, though."

"That's one of the things we love about it. You see, our milk—" Jason stopped himself mid-sentence. "What am I thinking? I was about to reveal all the secrets when you've only just arrived. Let's save it for the tour."

"Sounds good to me," I said, putting down the cockroach milk and picking up my coffee. Bill gave me a look that told me he was pleased with me for tasting the milk.

"Now, let's not forget we're here for a reason," Bill said, bringing a touch of seriousness to the proceedings.

"Of course," Jason said. "How would you like this visit to proceed?"

"We're anticipating our visit will take a few days. You mentioned something about a tour—that would be perfect. We were hoping we'd kick off the visit that way."

"Great minds think alike, Bill. I was planning to take you on the tour first thing today."

Bill nodded. "Good. After that, we will want to talk to some of your employees and, in all honesty, poke around the place for a while and see where our inspection takes us."

"That's totally fine by me. Treat every door as if it's open. We have nothing to hide."

During their conversation, my attention had been drawn to a map of the Insectalat site hanging on the wall.

"Is that where we are now?" I said, pointing to the largest building on the map.

"That's right."

"Is this an old map?"

"Why do you ask?"

"I saw another warehouse on the way in this morning. On the hill behind this building. It's missing from this map."

Jason looked at Bill and smiled. "She's good, Bill. I guess in your line of work, it's all about attention to detail."

Bill nodded. "Something like that."

Then Jason turned back to me. "You're right, Polly. That warehouse was built since this map was printed. That building is still a work in progress—no day-to-day operations take place in there yet."

"I'm sure our inspection of this building will give us everything we need," Bill said.

I was surprised by his words. His attitude seemed to be in direct conflict with everything I had been taught during my induction. As FDA inspectors, our jurisdiction stretched across any facility that could affect the quality and safety of the products. There was no question that a building barely a stone's throw from the main warehouse could have some kind of influence over the manufacturing process, no matter how many checks and balances the management think they have in place. For example, a rodent infestation in an adjacent building could easily result in contamination of the output of the building next door.

I decided to let it go. This was not the situation to assert what little authority I had. We would be there for a few days; there would be other opportunities to bring up the subject of the building on the hill.

Jason clapped his hands together and said, "Why don't I give you the tour?"

Chapter 14

A wall of noise and a thick, unholy stench hit me like a one-two punch in the face as I took my first step onto the factory floor. The sensory input was overwhelming, and I stood rooted to the spot in awed silence, trying to make sense of the scene before me.

I had visited manufacturing plants before and, just like the others, this one appeared impossible to understand at first glance. The combination of people pushing buttons and turning handles, complex machinery spinning and clanking, all servicing items creeping along a perpetually moving line, was both confusing and impressive at the same time. To an outsider, it was too much to take in, but to every individual on the factory floor, they knew their jobs exactly and were performing their specific role with the grace and efficiency that comes with well-organised, repetitive work.

"Impressive, isn't it?" Bill said.

"I'm always impressed by production lines," I said. "All this effort to produce a carton of blue milk."

Jason laughed. "Trust me, every step in this process is essential to the manufacturing process. I know it looks daunting, but everything here makes perfect sense in its own special way."

"I don't see any cockroaches," I said. "Not on the production line, or any escapees running around on the floor. Where are they?"

"That's a great question," Jason said. "In truth, no cockroaches make it onto the factory floor."

My face must have contorted into a picture of confusion, because Jason immediately responded with, "Not *living* cockroaches, anyway."

"You kill them first as part of the manufacturing process?"

"We have to. You see, the milk isn't exactly what you think. Cockroaches don't produce milk in liquid form that we can extract by attaching tiny tubes to them and hooking them up to a milking machine."

"That makes sense," I said. "I just hadn't thought about it until now."

"I'm sure most people in this world would be happy to live their entire lives without knowing how we produce this milk, which is why we don't make too much fanfare about it. We are confident in our product, and our marketing department appreciates the separation between the product and its origins."

"I can understand that. So, what is the milk and how do you extract it?"

"Female cockroaches create milk in the form of tiny crystals, which contain extremely concentrated quantities of energy and amino acids. Unfortunately, there is no way to extract those crystals without killing the cockroaches. The room where cockroaches are loaded onto the production line is off the main factory floor, partly for health and safety reasons—to contain any escapees—but also for psychological reasons. We found it unnecessary for the staff on the production line to witness the death of millions of cockroaches all day every day. I'd be happy to show you that point on the production line, though."

"I don't think—" Bill began, but I cut him off without thinking.

"Yes," I said. "I think we should see the entire production line from beginning to end."

For a split second, Jason and Bill shared a look.

"You heard the lady," Bill said with a shrug. "Let's see the killing room."

"Very good. Follow me."

The killing room was behind a locked door. Jason had been escorting us through every other door in the building by swiping his security pass, but this one was secured by a physical lock and key. He swung the door open and I let out an audible gasp at the sight before me.

"Impressive, isn't it?" Jason said.

"I can see why you keep this in a separate room."

With bare stone walls and floor, the room was large and most of the space within it was taken up by an enormous glass funnel. It must have been at least twenty feet tall, approximately the same in diameter, and it was filled all the way to the ceiling with live cockroaches. The swirling, writhing brown mass within the funnel was both disgusting and mesmerising.

At the base of the funnel was a six-foot metal cube. Every few seconds, the cube emitted a loud crunch, then dumped a quantity of tiny particles onto a conveyor belt, contained within a glass tube. Around the point of impact, the inside of the glass tube was stained brown with tiny pieces of the billions of mashed-up cockroaches that had passed through it.

"Don't tell me," I said, "you have a breeding room upstairs that feeds directly into the opening at the top."

"Right again! Bill, are you sure you haven't been giving away all our secrets?"

Bill shook his head. "Not a thing, Jason."

"Now, I could show you the breeding room, but I'm eager to press forward on the production line so you can see how we get from here to a carton of delicious milk at the end. Is that okay with you?"

I heard his words but took a few seconds too long to answer. I was hypnotised by the writhing mass of cockroaches waiting to meet their doom.

"What? Oh, yes," I said, snapping out of my trance. "I would like to see everything I can before we leave, though."

"Of course," Jason said, and led us back onto the main factory floor.

We followed as he talked us through each step on the production line. The mashed cockroaches emerged from the killing room through a hole in the wall and continued their journey, where they fell off the end of the conveyor belt into metal scoops that travelled upwards, to be dumped into a second huge funnel-shaped device. This time the funnel was solid steel, and it made a loud whirr as it vibrated.

"This is the separator," Jason said. "Because we're only interested in the crystals, we have to separate them from the rest of the cockroach carcass."

"How does it work?" I asked.

"That's our secret sauce," Jason said with a sly grin. "This machine is what allows us to do what all of our competitors find it impossible to do—easily separate enough crystals to produce cockroach milk on an industrial scale."

"So, you're saying you can't tell me?"

"In all honesty, I can't say for sure. I know it contains a complicated set of filters that somehow magically separate the crystals from the other bits of cockroach, but I'd be lying if I said I could tell you exactly how it works."

"It doesn't bother you that you don't know how the most important piece of equipment in your factory works?"

Jason shrugged. "I've got a computer on my desk. I don't know how that works, either. All I know is that when I hit the power button, it springs into life and does its thing. The same could be said for the separator."

"But I bet you keep someone around who knows how to fix your computer when it breaks."

Jason nodded.

"So, who fixes the separator when it breaks? Could we talk to them if we wanted to?"

"It's never broken down. If it ever did, we've got a number to call at head office. They would send someone along to take a look at it."

"But surely that means you'd need to shut the whole line down until it got fixed."

For the first time that morning, Jason's demeanour hardened. "Company policy," he said. "Lucky for us that the separator has never broken down, so we've never had to shut the line down."

"Never?"

He shook his head. "Not one minute."

"I'd love to know more about the separator," I said. "Maybe we could have a call with someone from head office, if they have the people in the know."

"Maybe," Jason said. I caught him glancing in Bill's direction, with an expression that I chose to interpret as, *why did you have to bring* her *with you?*

"Now, let's return to the production line," he said. "As you can see, there are two outputs from the separator."

Jason showed us how the ninety-nine percent of the cockroach carcasses that weren't needed were transported from the separator on a metal chute that left the machine about halfway up. A second, much smaller, metal chute at the bottom of the separator was waiting to receive regular deposits of a light blue powder.

"There we have it," he said, pointing at the sparkling blue powder as it moved past us. "The crystals that form the basis of the best superfood in the world."

"What happens to all the bits of cockroach you have left over?" I asked, pointing to the first metal chute.

"We don't let anything go to waste," he said. "The crushed-up pieces are taken away, packed into bags, and sold on."

"Who's buying crushed-up cockroaches?"

"You'd be surprised. I'm sure you're aware of the growing market in insect-based foodstuffs?"

I nodded.

"Well, the cockroaches you see here could quite easily be served up to you in a protein shake, granola, or the different types of 'bug burger' that are on the market right now."

"I've seen the ads. I have to be honest—I've never felt like trying any of them."

"You're missing out!" Jason exclaimed. I wondered whether there was ever a time when he wasn't in full salesman mode. Did he go home and tell his wife what he really thought about the strange things that rolled off his production line? Or was he a company man right down to his core?

"Now, let's follow the trail of crystals."

Jason led us across the factory floor, alongside the blue crystals as they made their way towards another piece of giant machinery. This metallic contraption was shaped like a barrel, with the feed of blue crystals entering through a tube at the top, next to a second metal tube. At the bottom of the barrel, blue milk flowed out through a glass tube, which ran along what remained of the factory floor and through the wall at the end.

"So this is where the crystals get turned into milk?" I said.

"That's right," Jason said. "This is the mixer. Crystals and water go in, some magic happens inside, and our special blended milk comes out at the bottom. Then it goes along that tube and into the bottling room."

I looked back at the production line, taking in the manufacturing process: the crusher, the separator, then the mixer. Factory workers dressed in white coats and hair nets monitored each station along the production line, checking monitoring screens and pressing buttons.

"What do you think so far?" Jason asked. "Impressive, huh?"

I nodded, still considering my response. "It's impressive that you have found a way to mass-produce something, where all of your competitors have failed," I began.

"Thank you. We're very proud—"

I cut him off mid-sentence. "But what is probably most impressive is the fact that the whole process is so simple."

His face contorted into a mixture of confusion and offence. "Simple?" he exclaimed, spitting the word at me. "You call this simple?" Then he took a moment to compose himself before continuing. "I'm sure our research and development team would convince you otherwise."

"I'm sorry," I said, without being sorry at all, "what I meant is that your production line is relatively straightforward, from a process perspective. There are only three main stations along the line before you get to bottling: crushing, filtering, and mixing. The technology you have developed at each station must be cutting edge to allow you to achieve what you have."

"I see what you mean," Jason said, shooting a glance in Bill's direction, who was choosing to remain silent throughout this exchange. "You are correct, of course. Please forgive my outburst; we're very protective of our technology and very proud of what we do here."

"I can see that," I said, "and so you should be."

Jason's salesman smile returned, but still his eyes burned into mine. I had lifted the veil for a second. *Is there more to find under there?* I wondered.

"Can we see the bottling room?" I asked.

"Of course. Follow me."

He led the way to a door next to the spot on the wall where the tube of blue milk disappeared. He swiped his security pass and opened the door to reveal a production line covering at least the same floor space as the one we had just left, if not more. We followed as he pointed at the machines and told us what they all did, but I found the bottling room far less intriguing than the manufacturing part of the tour.

In fact, the manufacturing floor became even more intriguing the more I came to understand the bottling process. Throughout the rest of the morning, it became clear that where the manufacturing process could be broken down into three very simple steps—crushing, filtering, and mixing—the bottling process was far more complex. The architects of this part of the production line seemed to have paid far more attention to the minute details, like the way the right number of bottles and cartons move along the line to be filled, sealed, labelled, and packed, than they had paid to the bang-bang-bang approach to manufacturing. Even the people working on the line seemed to be more attentive, as if a mistake in the bottling process would have far greater consequences than a mistake in manufacturing.

There were no surprises on this part of the tour, and I could tell Jason was going through the motions rather than singing the praises of the process and its associated technology like he had next door. The final stop was the loading bay, where the workers loaded pallets laden with cartons onto trucks that drove away, taking their orders out into the world, to the shops that sold this insane superfood to the crazy members of the public who thought it was a good idea to drink cockroach milk.

As we watched a truck leave the loading bay, Jason clapped his hands and said, "Okay, I think it's time for lunch."

Chapter 15

With a strange cocktail of hunger and apprehension in my stomach, I entered the cockroach milk factory canteen. At first glance, I saw that the place was busy, with very few spaces at the large number of tables. Then I noticed the line for food was empty.

"They say there's no such thing as a free lunch," Jason said with a knowing smile, "but that's not true here."

"That's usually true," I said as I grabbed a tray. "Where's the rub?"

"Keep an open mind," Bill said under his breath.

I pushed my tray to the serving station, where a man in catering overalls asked me what I'd like to eat. I asked him what they had, and he pointed out each dish in front of him.

"Pasta carbonara, burgers, or chilli."

I scanned the options in front of me. The burgers looked odd; not like any meat I'd seen before.

"What kind of meat is in the burgers?"

He exchanged a look with Jason, then said, "They're bug burgers, miss."

"Oh," I said. I was about to ask for the pasta instead when I thought it best to delve deeper. "Do you—"

He cut me off, like he was answering the same question for the millionth time in his life. "No, miss, we don't have anything that doesn't have bugs in it."

Jason chipped in. "I recommend the carbonara. It's made with our own milk, straight off the production line."

I looked again at the pasta and saw that the creamy sauce had a strange blue tint. Burgers and pasta were out of the question, but I was starving; I had to eat something.

"I'll have the chilli," I said. The man served me a bowl of rice with a big dollop of chilli on top. The sight of familiar ingredients like kidney beans pleased me, but I feared what horrors were lurking within the sauce. I placed the bowl of chilli on my tray and grabbed a large bottle of water to wash it down with. Jason chose the pasta and Bill opted for the burger, then we found the sole empty table in the far corner of the canteen. On my journey through the maze of tables and chairs, I spotted very few trays of food like ours; most of the staff were eating from lunch boxes they'd brought in from home. My analysis of the situation told me the people reluctantly picking at bug pasta, bug chilli, and bug burgers were new to the company today, and they were now determined to bring their own lunch tomorrow.

We sat down, and I sat with my fork hovering over my bowl of chilli. My lunch stared back at me. I could hear its voice, taunting me.

I know I look like a regular bowl of chilli, but I'm full of mashed-up pieces of cockroach and you have to eat me because those two men are watching you. Go on, just stick your fork into me and take a big bite.

"It won't kill you, you know," Jason said, making me jump as his words snapped me out of my trance. "You never know, you might like it!"

My only reply was to scoop up a big forkful and shovel it into my mouth, preparing myself for the worst. It tasted just like chilli and had the same texture, too. My mind had convinced me that I would be left with a cockroach's leg stuck between my teeth, but on first impression, this was indistinguishable from regular chilli. It could have been a bit spicier, but wasn't that always the case with workplace food?

"Well, what's the verdict?" Jason asked.

I offered him another wordless reply: a thumbs-up with my left hand while I took another bite with my right. It was the best show of defiance I could come up with.

"Told you!" he said, then turned his attention to Bill, who was sitting next to me. "You didn't hang around!"

I turned to see Bill stuffing the last piece of his burger into his mouth, then he got to his feet, announcing, "I'm going back for seconds."

"Be my guest," Jason said, watching as Bill headed for the non-existent serving line. "There goes a man who likes his food."

With Bill out of earshot, I found myself with an opportunity.

"What's your take on the man who went missing?"

Jason's eyes darted to Bill, as if he was calculating how long it would take for him to return.

"His name was Alistair Cameron—Al to his friends."

"Were you one of his friends?"

"Not at all," Jason said. "Honestly? He was a pain in the ass, one of those employees every boss gets from time to time; the type who complains about anything and everything."

"What would he complain about?"

"Shift patterns, pay, benefits, healthcare, equipment. Everything. You want to know what I think?"

Polly nodded.

"I think he just up and left town. He was always making noises about quitting. He never did enough to make it easy for me to fire him, though. He was good enough at his job, just a pain in the ass to deal with. Out of everyone here, I'd put him down as the most likely just to disappear without telling anyone."

"He must have had friends here, though?"

"Of course," Jason said. He was about to say more, but I saw his eyes dart to the side, then he checked himself. Bill arrived, carrying a plate loaded up with bug pasta.

"We were just talking about our missing employee," Jason announced, and Bill shot me with a look that told me two things. One: he knew I was the one who had raised the point. Two: he was unhappy with me for doing so.

"And what conclusion did you come to?" Bill asked.

"It seems possible that he just stopped turning up for work," I conceded.

Jason and Bill both smiled and nodded, apparently pleased with my reading of the situation.

"But," I continued, "it would be good to talk to one or two of his friends."

Jason and Bill's eyes met.

"After all, we'll need to talk to a selection of employees as part of the inspection anyway, won't we?"

"Of course," Jason said. "I'll check the rota to see when Al's closest friends are due on shift."

"That'll be fine," Bill said, then began shovelling bug pasta into his mouth.

Chapter 16

After lunch, Bill left me with Jason while he disappeared into an office, saying he was going to talk to the health and safety officer. With the morning's tour of the facility out of the way, it was time for the inspection to begin. This meant I had to put some of my personalities on hold and focus on just one of them. In order to do my job as an inspector for the FDA, I felt like I had to forget I was an undercover operative for the Resistance, and that I was also a concerned citizen who had been attacked by an overgrown cockroach in a public toilet. I was Polly Benton, FDA Inspector, and I had to allocate all my brain power to recalling my training and applying it to the job immediately in front of me.

Jason suggested that we begin in the bottling room. It seemed like the most straightforward operation and felt representative of many similar operations I might be asked to inspect in my time with the FDA, so I had no objections. It also meant I would be putting off the inspection of the filtering room until the next morning, something I was more than happy to do. I had seen enough pieces of mashed-up cockroach for one day.

I worked my way along the bottling line one piece of equipment at a time, taking swabs of surfaces as I went, labelling the samples and securing them in my backpack. When these samples went off to the FDA lab for testing at the end of our inspection, I felt confident they would all come back negative. The surfaces along the bottling line were spotless, which was no surprise given all the cleaning activity going on around me. After the shock and awe brought about by the killing, crushing, and filtering, I feel no shame in admitting that I switched off in the bottling room during that part of the tour that morning. Now that I had to spend several hours in there, it was only natural to pay attention to everything that was going on. When I stopped to watch the people around me, it seemed like every other person was scrubbing, wiping, or polishing the floor or the machinery.

"I must say I'm very impressed by the cleaning effort going on here," I remarked to Jason.

"Thank you," he said. "We're very proud of our efforts. I'm talking about everything: our technology, our production line, and, of course, our hygiene efforts."

"We always expect to see a ramp-up in cleaning whenever we launch an inspection, but this is so far over and above what I might expect that I'm finding it difficult to be cynical about it. I suspect it would be very difficult to round up such a large number of cleaning contractors at the short notice we gave you before we arrived."

"Your reading of the situation is correct, Polly. We know that, given what we do here, our operation is naturally going to be subject to increased scrutiny. One mistake is going to put our entire business in jeopardy. We believe in what we do here. We believe the products we produce are critical to the future of the human race, to the sustainability of the food sources we have on this planet. We believe one mistake puts our future at risk."

I was taken aback at the conviction in his words. This wasn't sales patter; he really meant what he was saying. "I believe you," I said.

I took a final swab, labelled the container, and placed it in my backpack, then made a show of checking the time on my watch. It was just after six o'clock. "I think that'll do for today," I said.

"Excellent. I look forward to seeing you again in the morning. I'll take you round the first half of the production line tomorrow."

"Sounds good," I said. "It would also be good if we could get a tour of the rest of the facility, including the building on the hill."

A dark cloud swept across Jason's eyes. "Maybe," he said. "Let's see how much time we have tomorrow."

"It's okay. We've got all the time in the world."

For the first time since I had met him, Jason appeared to be forcing a smile. "Have a good evening, Polly. I believe your colleague has already left. I'll call you a cab."

Chapter 17

I needed a beer. Despite my run-in with the giant cockroach the night before, I felt the draw of the bar across the road from the motel. Being conscious that some of the people in the bar might be the same people working on the line I had been inspecting, I changed out of my work clothes and into something more comfortable, not wishing to draw attention to the narc sitting by herself in the corner.

As I left my room, I thought I should make an attempt at building bridges with my colleague. The problem was that I didn't know which room Bill was staying in, so I didn't know which door to knock on. I dug my phone out of my bag, intending to send him a message, but found one from him waiting for me.

Heading to the bar over the road for a beer and to arrest the cockroach who attacked you. Maybe see you there.

He had sent it ten minutes ago, while I was getting changed. I crossed the road and entered the bar, finding it just as busy as it had been the night before. The big screens were still tuned to ESPN, this time showing a bunch of men in suits behind a desk talking about the upcoming Super Bowl.

Bill was at the front of the crush at the bar, and he spotted me just as he was getting served. Over the noise of the bar, he mouthed "What do you want?" to me, and I mouthed "Beer and chicken wings" back at him, which he acknowledged with a thumbs-up. I found a table for two, and Bill came over a minute later with two big frozen glasses of foaming beer. We clinked glasses and took a drink. It was cold and bitter, and felt fantastic.

"So that's day one of inspection number one done," Bill said. "How does it feel?"

"It feels good," I said, feeling confident in the thought that I'd done a good job.

"You did a good job today," he said. "Maybe asking a few too many pointed questions for your first day at a site, but that's a common thing for a newbie."

"Okay," I said, then reflected on the conversations I'd had with Jason the factory manager. "You mean the questions I was asking about the guy who went missing?"

Bill nodded. "And the building on the hill."

"What would you do? We can't let things like that slide."

"I know, but we're here for a few days. On most inspections, you'll find you have time to build a bit of a rapport with the people on site. It's easier to make friends with them and let them tell you what you want to know, rather than shining a light in their face and shouting 'Confess!' as soon as you step out of the taxi."

That made me laugh. "I know I wasn't quite that bad."

"Okay, maybe not, but I feel like it's my duty to offer you some constructive feedback."

"Constructive feedback, eh? Very corporate."

"Looks who's talking," he said.

I felt my face flush, the way it always did when I knew I was about to get drawn into a conversation about my time at Synergy Services.

"You've done your research, then?" I said.

"Of course. Unless your name's something like John Smith, there's no hiding from a Google search."

"Well, now you know that I'm a millionaire, I don't want to be accused of being a cheapskate. I'll pick up the tab."

Bill laughed. "It's okay. It's all going on expenses."

"Well, now you know about me, you need to tell me something about you."

"Okay," Bill said, taking another gulp of beer, "what do you want to know?"

"How long have you worked for the FDA?"

"All my working life," he said with a sigh. "First job was an office admin, then I worked my way up to inspector and decided to stay there."

"Why didn't you want to take it any further?"

"Travelling all over the country isn't conducive to a happy family life, but I don't have a family and I enjoy travelling."

"So do you not have a family because you enjoy the job, or do you do enjoy the job because you don't have a family?"

"Some days it's one of the above, some days it's the other."

Our food arrived and we began tucking in, then I asked the question I'd been dying to ask all day, with as much nonchalance as I could muster.

"How many times have you visited the Insectalat factory before?"

Bill looked up with genuine surprise at my question. "What makes you think I've been there before?"

Anticipating that kind of response, I had already rehearsed the answer in my mind. "I just assumed you and Jason knew each other, from the way you were together."

For a couple of seconds, I watched the gears of Bill's brain turn, quickly processing all the information available to him to form a coherent response. Then he smiled and said, "You're good, Polly. Very perceptive. You'll do well at the FDA. I bet when you get a hunch about something, you're nearly always right, aren't you?"

I nodded. "I got a hunch about you today. And you haven't answered the question. How many times have you visited the factory before?"

"I've lost count," he said, without missing a beat. "So now you're wondering why I wouldn't tell you I'd been there before, whether I'm hiding something from you?"

"Pretty much."

Bill shook his head. "There was no benefit in telling you whether I'd been there before or not."

"Why?"

"You're new to all this. You need to learn. If you think the older guy you're with knows much more than you, you'll clam up and let me take the lead. You won't learn as much, and you won't get the opportunity to apply what they taught you in your induction training."

I wanted to protest, but I didn't know what I was protesting, other than the feeling that Bill hadn't been honest with me.

"This isn't a sexism thing, in case you're wondering," he said. "I do this with every new recruit I get paired up with: male, female, and all the shades of grey in between that we seem to have these days. Everyone who's served their time does it too, including the women. As a matter of fact, you're lucky you didn't get paired up with one of the women. Most of them are total bitches."

I reeled in shock at his words.

"You don't believe me?" he laughed. "Wait until you get paired up with a few of them. Then come and find me and tell me what you think. I should know—my sister was one of those bitches."

"Was?"

"Well, she still *is* a bitch, just not for the FDA. She spent a few years paying her dues in the public sector, then jumped ship the second her dream job came along."

"What was that?"

"A pencil pusher in the White House, but she's moving up in the world now that the administration's changing."

"She worked for President Green?"

Bill nodded. "It wouldn't surprise me if she had a hand in his assassination."

"You don't mean that," I said, hoping the conversation wasn't about to take a darker turn.

He laughed. "No, of course not. But I wouldn't want to cross her. From what she tells me, Washington politics is pretty cut-throat, and you need to be tough to get through it. Mind you, you'd know about that, wouldn't you?"

"I've seen a little of what goes on, yes, and that's enough for one lifetime, as far as I'm concerned."

"We don't see each other much, but from what she tells me, I think I can understand why you wanted to distance yourself from all that."

"Okay, so now that we've got to know each other a bit more, I've got another question for you."

"Go ahead."

"You don't seem that concerned about the guy who went missing from the factory. I mean, that's the reason we're here. Why is that?"

Bill shrugged. "We're here to do a job. That job is to carry out an inspection. Yes, the inspection may have been prompted by a man's disappearance, but the work we're here to do remains the same, irrespective of what brought us here."

"You're not interested in finding out what happened to him?"

"Maybe I would have been when I was in your position. But now? No, not really. Get ready, Polly, because I'm going to pass on some words of wisdom that were given to me when I was just starting off as an inspector. Ready?"

I nodded.

"You work for the FDA, not the FBI. You're here to find out if the food production and cleaning processes meet standards, not to play Nancy Drew."

"I guess you're right," I admitted. "But I can't help being curious."

"That's good, and don't lose that curiosity, but apply it in the right places. If you go looking for things we're not here to find, that's where you'll get into trouble."

We finished our meals, then Bill looked at me and said, "What do you say we exercise that curiosity of yours and see if we can find that monster cockroach that attacked you last night?"

I opened the door to the ladies' bathroom and confirmed the coast was clear. Bill followed me inside.

"Where did you see it last night?" he said.

"Right there," I said, pointing to the spot underneath the sink. "First of all, a regular-sized cockroach came out from that crack in the wall, then the monster appeared and attacked it. It looked like it started to eat it."

Bill knelt and examined the spot on the floor under the sink. "It looks clean down here."

I scanned the bathroom. "Now that you mention it, it looks a lot cleaner in here than it did last night."

"Maybe it was cleaning day today."

"If that's the case, then I think cleaning day comes round maybe once a month, at most."

"And this is the hole they came through?" Bill said, moving over to the wall. He examined the crack, then took out his phone, turned on the flashlight, and shone it inside.

He turned to me and said, "It's been filled in."

"Really?"

"Take a look," he said, and handed me his phone as he got to his feet. I knelt and shone the light into the crack. Bill was right; the crack in the wall had been filled in with sealant. I prodded a finger inside.

"It's still soft."

"They probably filled it in just before they opened for the evening."

I got to my feet and handed Bill's phone back to him. "They knew we were on to them," I said.

"That's a fair assumption," he said. "Seems logical that any one of the people we met today would have tipped off the owner of their favourite watering hole about the FDA being in town."

"Anything we can do about this?" I asked, feeling deflated.

"Not right now. Best we can do is recommend an inspection in a couple of months' time. They might think they've patched up the problem, but if those roaches want to get in, they'll find another way. Then we'll have someone here to shut them down."

"Is that all we can do?"

Bill shrugged.

"It doesn't help us explain one thing, though."

"What's that?"

"What happened to cause that cockroach to grow so massive in the first place."

Bill laughed. "I was wrong about you."

"How?"

"I called you Nancy Drew earlier. I should have called you Agent Scully."

Part 4: Wednesday 22nd January

Chapter 18

My second day at the factory began with the inspection of the filtering room. Bill made some passing comment about checking the cleaning records when we arrived, then disappeared, leaving me under the supervision of the ever-grinning Jason.

"Is there a particular reason why this room is so different from the bottling room?" I asked him.

"What makes you say that?"

"Well, I was in the bottling room all afternoon yesterday and I got the sense that you pay great attention to cleanliness and maintenance of the machinery in there."

"I sense a 'but' coming," he said.

"But it's a different story in here."

"How so?"

"It feels like there is a general lack of attention to detail in here, certainly in comparison to the bottling room. I took dozens of samples from various surfaces in the bottling room yesterday, and I don't think you'll be surprised if I tell you I'm expecting them all to come back from the lab saying everything is clean."

"You're right; I won't be surprised at that."

"But in here, everything seems to be coated in a layer of dust, thin in some places that are probably given a cursory wipe with a cloth once a day, but thick in harder-to-reach places that I suspect aren't part of a cleaning regime at all. Now that I think about it, I've been in here all morning and I haven't seen anyone pushing a mop and bucket around, but there seemed to be a permanent cleaning operation running in the bottling room."

Jason, who was still smiling, put his hands together as if he was praying and asked, "Anything else?"

"There's nowhere near as many staff in here, and I have to say their attitude is very different to their colleagues next door."

"Their attitude?"

"Look around," I said. We took a moment to cast our eyes around the filtering room. I counted only a handful of staff, some of them wearing torn and dirty white coats, and others who hadn't even bothered to follow the instructions on the door to the room telling them to wear protective clothing at all times. Some had protective plastic glasses perched on their heads, and others hadn't bothered picking up a pair. Most of them had their hands in their pockets, pacing back and forth as if they were killing time, waiting for their shift to end.

"Do you see what I mean?" I asked. "The men and women next door seemed like they were paying far more attention to detail."

Jason paused for a moment, then leaned in close and lowered his tone of voice, almost to a whisper. "Thank you for raising this. I was hoping you would pick up on this and put it in your report."

"Really?" I said.

"That's the reason I asked for the inspection."

"*You* asked for the inspection?"

"That's right. It's not really got anything to do with our man who disappeared. That was just convenient timing. You see, I've been desperate to make changes to the filtering room for a long time. We need a full change of staff and we need new machinery that's more reliable. Head office doesn't want to hear anything about it. They refuse to invest any more money in this operation."

"So, you were hoping that if an FDA inspection revealed some serious problems, they would have no choice but to give you the investment to make the changes?"

"Exactly!"

"But what about the man who disappeared?"

"What about him?"

"Aren't you worried? One of your employees is missing."

Jason laughed, like I'd just said the most absurd thing in the world. "Look," he began, "employees come and go here. If I asked the cops to send out a search party every time someone didn't turn up to work, they'd lock *me* up. Al hated working here—he made no secret of it—but the money was good. He used to tell his colleagues that one day he'd tell me to stick my job where the sun don't shine."

"And did he?"

"As a matter of fact, he did."

"Really? When?"

"The day before he left. You see, Polly, there really isn't any scandal. It happens a lot here. Maybe it's because our line of business is a little strange. Maybe it's because we're only a stone's throw from Roswell, which brings out all the conspiracy theorists. Either way, we know there will always be questions hanging over what we do here, and there's nothing we can do about that. One thing I can do is tell you there's no problem with Al's disappearance. He quit, and now he's probably moved on to another job in another town."

I said nothing. I was struggling to process Jason's words against everything I had seen, everything I had heard, and my unfounded suspicions over the last few days.

"Now," Jason said, "you wanted to speak to one of Al's friends, didn't you?"

I nodded.

"Wes was probably his best friend here, and he's on shift today. Do you still want to speak to him, or have you heard enough from me?"

I was on the verge of accepting Jason's version of events so I could finish up and get out of there, but something inside wouldn't let me give in.

"I should speak to him while I've got the chance," I said. "Just to get the full picture."

"Of course," Jason said. "If you come to my office after lunch, I'll bring him to you."

I thanked Jason, then we finished the morning's checks in the filtering room and went for lunch. Like all right-minded people on their second day at the Insectalat factory, I had brought my own.

Chapter 19

Jason showed Wes into the office. We shook hands and he sat down, then Jason closed the door behind him as he left. I recognised Wes; he had arrived for the start of his shift just as I was finishing up for lunch. He had the same weary look of the other people who worked in the filtering room. I estimated his age at early forties, but there was something about this place that seemed to mask a person's real age.

"Thank you for coming in to talk to me," I said.

Wes shrugged. "I get paid whether I'm in here or down there. In here is as good as a break, so I should be thanking you. The boss said you're here from the FDA."

"That's right."

"Never seen anyone come in here off the line to talk to the FDA before."

"Really?"

Wes nodded. "And you guys are here all the time. You're new, though? New here, at least."

"Yes, this is my first time visiting this facility," I said, trying to process his words and formulate a measured response. "So you've seen inspectors from the FDA here before?"

"Oh yeah. I saw another guy on the way in today. I guess he's with you? I know he's FDA because I've seen him a bunch of times."

"Recently?" I asked.

"Oh yeah. I last seen him, hmm, maybe a month ago? Then the month before that, and the month before that."

"How long have you worked here, Wes?"

"A couple of years now, pretty much since it opened."

I felt like any more questions on this subject would draw attention to the fact that I was pursuing an investigation outside of my FDA jurisdiction.

"Well, I'm here to conduct a regular investigation, so I have just a few standard questions to ask you. Is that okay?"

"Are you going to do anything about Al?"

Wes' response caught me off guard. "You're talking about the man who was reported missing?"

"Yeah. I'm the one who reported him missing."

"I heard that he quit, that he'd been threatening to quit for a while."

"Nah, that's all bull, lady. Well, maybe not the threats to quit. That happens to all of us from time to time. See, we all know what goes on here, us in the filtering room. Al knew it and decided to find out a little bit more than the rest of us. The night he did, that was the night he went missing."

"What did he do, that night?"

"We finished our shift at midnight. We're heading outside when he says he wants to go up to the building on the hill."

"Have you ever been up there before?"

"No, ma'am."

"What goes on up there?"

"No one knows. No one who talks to us, anyway. Al says he's going to find out, and off he goes. I never saw him again. Never heard from him."

"You don't think he left town?"

"Nah, that's all bull, too. Al never left town. He never even made it home that night."

"What makes you so certain?"

"I've been round his place. Looked in the window. Everything's the same as he left it. Pictures of him and his buddies from the army still hanging on the wall. Anyone who knows Al knows he wouldn't split and leave stuff like that behind."

"So what are you saying? What do you think happened to him?"

"He went up the hill and never came back. Can't put it any simpler than that."

"What do you think goes on up there?"

"That's where the real work happens."

"What do you mean by that?"

Wes pushed his chair back and got to his feet. "It's easier if I show you. If I tell you first, you probably won't believe me."

Chapter 20

We returned to the production line and stood in front of the blue crystals that were flowing out of the filtering machine. Wes dug in his pockets and produced a coin, holding it up so I could see it.

"Just a regular quarter, right?" he said.

"What is this, a magic trick?" I said.

"Something like that."

Wes took a black marker out of his pocket and drew an X onto the quarter. He held it up in one hand, then took his phone out of another pocket and tapped at it for a few seconds. He looked over his shoulder as if he wanted to make sure no one was watching. Then he tapped his phone screen and threw the quarter into the crystals.

"What are you doing?" I exclaimed as the coin zipped along the conveyor towards the next machine. Wes said nothing.

"What are you trying to prove?" I said. "Won't that coin snarl up the machinery further down the line? What about cross-contamination? I'm going to find it very difficult not to put this in my report."

"Calm down, lady," he said. "I ain't cross-contaminating nothing."

Wes checked the screen of his phone, then searched around the racks of equipment and paperwork that ran along the side of the production line until he found what he was looking for: a net with a long handle, a larger version of the type of net used for cleaning out fish tanks. He positioned himself alongside the flow of crystals, net in one hand, phone in the other. His phone sounded its alarm tone. He tapped the screen to turn it off, then leaned towards the production line and lowered the net into the flowing crystals. After waiting a few seconds for the net to fill up, he lifted it out and brought it closer to inspect. He dug around in the crystals, then held up the quarter, which had the same X written on it in marker pen.

"I don't understand," I said. "How did you do that?"

"You seem like a clever lady," he said. "I'll give you a minute. I'm sure you'll work it out."

Wes tipped the crystals back into the flow and returned the net to the spot where he had found it. I watched the crystals flow past us and into the huge barrel-shaped machine further down the production line. Just like I had seen yesterday on Jason's tour, I watched crystals go in, along with pipes carrying water. At the bottom of the machine, blue cockroach milk flowed out through glass pipes, into the bottling room next door. My attention went back to the water pipes at the top of the machine. They were opaque. I only knew they contained water because that's what Jason told me. Now that I was paying more attention, I spotted another pipe coming out of the bottom of the mixing machine, which headed in the opposite direction. I side-stepped back along the production line, following the pipe as it snaked between the various machines and obstacles that seemed to have been placed strategically to obscure its existence. The pipe fed into the filtering machine.

"You got it, don't you?" Wes said.

"These crystals are fake," I said. "This part of the production line is just one big loop, sending the crystals round and round."

"Every sixty seconds," Wes said, holding up his phone to show that his countdown timer had been set to one minute. "Like clockwork."

"But this is the middle of the production line," I said. "If this is fake, then—"

"This whole room is fake," he said.

"But what about the killing room?"

"Same trick. How are you ever going to know whether the bugs in the machine are the same ones that supposedly get crushed? That's why they make that room so disgusting, so no one ever hangs around in there long enough to work out what's really going on."

I made my way back to the mixing machine. "So if those crystals aren't used to make the milk, then where does it come from?"

I followed the pipe that Jason had told me carried water into the machine. It stretched out towards the back of the warehouse and through the wall.

"Do you know where that pipe goes?"

Wes nodded. "It goes to the building on the hill."

I looked back down the length of the production line. "So this is all fake, right up to this point. The milk is real, so the bottling room is real. That explains why there are so many more people in there, why so much attention is paid to cleaning and keeping the machinery running."

"All that stepped up after the leak," Wes said.

"What leak?"

"I think it was about a year ago. There was a leak in the pipe right there, where it passes through the wall into the bottling room. Nobody spotted it for several days. Milk was leaking through the wall cavity and collecting in the foundations of the building. This happened at the same time that a bunch of roaches got out of the killing room. They got into cracks in the walls and found their way to where the milk was leaking. Turns out that when roaches drink that milk, they grow big. I'm talking *really* big."

"I've seen one!" I exclaimed. "There are still some out there."

"I know," Wes said. "I still see one of them every now and again. Mean bastards they are, too. You know what that tells me?"

I shook my head.

"Whatever's going on up at the building on the hill—whatever they're doing to make that milk—it ain't no tiny blue roach crystals they're using to do it."

"Someone here must know what goes on up there."

"Maybe they do, but they ain't talking. I don't know anyone who's been up there who's come back and talked about it."

"I'm going to find Jason," I said. "I'm going to insist he opens the place up for inspection."

Wes shook his head. "He ain't gonna do that. He'll find some reason not to do it, then you're on a plane back home and we're all still here bottling this blue milk coming from god knows what."

"So what do you suggest?"

"I get off shift at midnight," he said with a conspiratorial twinkle in his eye. "Let's go up there and find out what the hell is going on, once and for all."

Chapter 21

Wes went back to work. His "work," as I had now learned, was to be paid well over the norm for a regular factory job to look busy and keep his goddamn mouth shut. I finished up in the filtering room, doing little more than the absolute minimum to make it look like the place deserved genuine attention.

I turned his offer over and over in my mind. Come back here at midnight and go up to the building on the hill with him. And then what? Break in? Wait outside for someone to enter and sneak in behind them? For all I knew, I might not have the option. Bill might have booked us on the first flight out of Roswell as soon as we're done here, which would mean I couldn't do a thing about it. And even if we went up there, and we found something worthy of all this intrigue and apparent conspiracy, what could I actually do about it? The best I'd be able to do was call it in. And if I did, what would I put in my report? That I've found serious wrongdoing going on at the Insectalat plant, but don't pay any attention to my own wrongdoing that led to the discovery?

Best case: I find something worthy of reporting and I also find a way to tie it back to what I've seen on the inspection.

Worst case: Wes and I get arrested and convicted of breaking and entering.

The more I thought about it, the less compelling the case became for coming back here at midnight. But something inside me just wouldn't let it lie. Something just didn't feel right about what was going on here.

I was packing away my things when Bill came over to me wearing his coat, with his bag over his shoulder, and asked me how things were going.

"Good," I said. "You look like you're done for the day."

"Not just for the day," he said. "I think we're done here for good."

I suspected that would be his summary, but I did my best to look surprised. "Really? We haven't taken Jason up on the offer to see the breeding room or the other building."

"Which other building?"

"The one on the hill."

"Are you still doing the Agent Scully thing?" he asked with a smirk.

"I spoke to someone who knew the man who went missing."

"That sounds like a yes."

"He said Al went up to that building, and that was the last time he saw him."

"That might be true, but while you were playing FBI down here, I've been doing my own detective work, to satisfy your curiosity more than mine."

"Oh yeah?"

"Yeah. I checked the HR records for the guy who went missing."

"And?"

"If the company had wanted to get rid of him, they could have done it a long time ago. He had the worst sickness record of anyone on the production line, and the instances of insubordination and misconduct could have added up to dismissal long before he disappeared."

"So why didn't they get rid of him sooner? Why keep a problem employee around?"

Bill seemed surprised at my response. "So now you're saying they should have sacked him ages ago?"

"Yes, if what you're saying is true. Why keep him around unless they had some other reason to do so?"

"What are you saying, Polly?"

"I'm saying I think there are some people who work in this factory that know things that put the company in a difficult position. If they let them go, the secrecy they rely on is put at risk."

Bill opened his mouth to voice his rebuttal, then thought better of it. He thought for a moment. "Look," he said, "we're done here. You've taken all the samples you need. I've seen everything I need to see. As far as the FDA is concerned, we're done, and last time I checked, it was the FDA that paid our wages, not the FBI. Right?"

I shrugged my acknowledgement that Bill had successfully stated the obvious. I had heard everything

I needed to hear. Bill wasn't interested in pursuing that line of investigation, and he couldn't care less about the breeding room or the building on the hill. Wes was the only ally I had in the building.

"Come on," he said, "let's get out of here. You've had an interesting first assignment, but there's no great mystery to solve here. You've done your job, and you've done it well. Now we get to go back to the motel and pack, then get on the first flight back to D.C. in the morning."

We said our goodbyes to Jason, then got a taxi back to the motel. As Bill was paying the taxi driver, I went into the office to tell the manager we would be checking out in the morning, but as soon as he saw me coming, he reached under the desk and pulled out an envelope.

"I've got a message for you, ma'am," he said, thrusting the envelope in my direction. I looked at it for a split second before quickly folding it up and stuffing it in my pocket before Bill arrived. I looked over my shoulder and saw him start to emerge from the taxi.

"A courier delivered it this afternoon," the manager said. "He said it was urgent."

"Thank you," I said, trying to draw this event to a close before Bill arrived. "I just wanted to let you know we'll be checking out first thing."

"That's right," Bill said as he marched into the office. "Can we settle up tonight?"

"Sure," the manager said. "Do it now if you want. In the morning, just post your keys into the mailbox."

"You go up to your room," Bill said to me, "and I'll sort this out here. Want to eat over the road again?"

"Sure," I said. "Just knock when you're ready."

I left the office and let out a long breath of relief as I closed the door to my room behind me. I felt certain that Bill hadn't picked up on the message the manager had given me, but I had been seconds away from some awkward questions. I put my bag down in the corner, pulled the envelope out of my pocket, and sat down on the bed to read it.

The only writing on the envelope was my name. I tore it open and opened the single sheet of paper inside. The typed note read:

Polly,

Thank you for your report.

We have been wanting to get someone on the inside of the Insectalat factory for a long time. We believe there are things going on at the factory that Insectalat would not want to be made public. We are unsure of the nature of their actions, but we have reason to suspect they relate to our interests.

Please pursue all available lines of enquiry. Gather as much information as you can. Talk to as many people as you can. We await your next report with interest.

P.S. Destroy this note.

I tore the note and the envelope into thin strips as I walked to the bathroom. I threw them into the toilet and stared at them. I had been unsure of what to do, whether to push my investigation any further or to write off my bad feeling about the factory, ignore what Wes had shown me, and get back to work for the FDA on the other side of the country. This note from the Resistance made my mind up for me. I had no choice; I had to find a way to get over to the factory by midnight and join Wes on his mission. Another certainty was that Bill would not want to get involved and may even try to stop me if he got wind of what I was planning.

A knock at the door made me jump. I shouted, "Give me a minute," and Bill shouted, "Take your time," back through the door, followed by, "Tell you what, I'll see you over the road."

"Okay," I shouted back.

I flushed the toilet and watched the strips of paper disappear, then quickly changed into comfortable clothes and left the motel room. I had a few hours to kill, then I had to find my chance to sneak away without Bill noticing.

I stopped at two beers and drew the evening to a close just after ten. We went back to our rooms, with no plans other than the promise of calling for a taxi at six the next morning to take us to the airport. Or so Bill thought.

I spent the next hour fidgeting in the dark. I left the lights off, hoping to give any casual observers the impression I had gone off to sleep. This made me restless with nerves. I had no idea what to expect from the night ahead. I only knew one thing: this was the most un-Polly-like thing I had ever done. How had I got myself into this? My life was supposed to follow the predictable path of high school, college, job, career, then more career, and maybe a family along the way. But no, I had to go and make a deal with our corrupt government and flip the table on what was becoming a neatly laid life.

Oh well, I thought, *no sense in beating yourself up about it. It happened, and you can't change it. All you can do is suck it up and make the best of this weird situation.*

Chapter 22

I opened my eyes and was immediately overcome with confusion and panic.

What happened? Where am I?

Then the realisation hit me: I had fallen asleep. I checked the time. It was 11:43. I cursed myself and ran for the door, grabbing my jacket as I went. Despite my stupidity, Lady Luck must have been smiling on me, because I found a taxi sitting outside the bar, dropping off its last fare. A couple were waiting to get in, so I thrust a ten dollar bill in the hand of the woman and said, "Sorry, I'm in a rush, the next cab's on me," as I jumped in the back and slammed the door shut.

"Where to, lady?" the driver asked over his shoulder.

"Insectalat."

"The factory?"

"That's right."

"You late for work?"

"Something like that."

"No worries, lady. You ain't the first and you won't be the last. Don't worry, I'll get you there on time."

He wasn't lying. The cab ride was like a rollercoaster, but true to his word, we arrived at the entrance to the Insectalat plant at 11:56.

"That'll be eight fifty," he said.

"Here's a ten," I said, passing him the money. He thanked me for it, but I offered him more.

"Here's another ten for getting here so quick."

"Wow, thanks!"

"And here's a twenty."

"Whoa, what the hell is this for?"

"To forget this trip altogether."

He took the twenty and looked at it for a moment. "I feel like I'm gonna see somethin' on the news tomorrow, and I'll know it's you that's the reason for it bein' on the news."

"Maybe, maybe not," I said. "But if anyone comes round tomorrow asking you if you gave me a lift here tonight, what are you going to say?"

He folded up the twenty and popped it into his shirt pocket. "I'm gonna say I don't remember. I take people to and from this place all the time. I'll tell 'em last night wasn't no different."

"That's good enough for me," I said as I opened the door. "Have a good night."

"You too. Whatever you're into, good luck with it. Hope I don't see you on the news."

Me too, I thought as I got out. I checked my watch: two minutes until the late shift was due to end. I'd made it on time. I approached the main entrance of the factory and waited in the shadows for Wes to appear. At midnight, the doors swung open and a swarm of factory workers flooded out, most of them heading for the parking lot, bus stop, or the line of cabs, but a few stopped to light a cigarette. I spotted Wes among them.

I watched him get a light from one of his co-workers, inhaling deeply, enjoying that first hit of nicotine in hours. I stepped forward out of the shadow. He gave me a nod of acknowledgement and made his way over.

"Didn't think you'd come," he said.

"I nearly didn't," I said, "but my curiosity got the better of me."

He took another deep drag on his cigarette, then exhaled the smoke from the side of his mouth, away from me. "You know what they say about curiosity."

"You think that's what killed your friend?

Wes nodded.

"And you still want to go up there?"

"I feel like I got no choice," Wes said. "I gotta find out what happened to Al. It's driving me crazy not knowing."

We both turned to look at the building on the hill. It felt as if the lighting had been made gloomier up there on purpose, to cast a spectre over the place, to deter any snoopers. But the effect was the opposite. I felt as if the building was drawing me towards it, as if there was a sign at the entrance that read, "Bad stuff is going on up here. Visit us at your peril."

A pair of headlights appeared in the darkness. We watched in silence as they headed towards the building on the hill.

"There," Wes said. "Most nights, at midnight, a truck goes up there."

"What's inside it?"

"No idea. The night Al disappeared, a truck went up there and he ran off to find out what was going on. Never saw him again."

"And you're planning to do the same?"

Wes shrugged. "You got a better plan?"

Chapter 23

We walked up the path towards the building on the hill with as much nonchalance as we could muster, as if our journey was the most logical thing in the world. To a casual observer, it was only natural for these two people to be walking from one building to the other at this time of night. Move along, nothing to see here. In truth, my heart was pounding in my chest, and in the low light I saw the muscles in Wes's jaw clenching with worry.

As we approached, we saw a set of shutters open up to allow the truck to reverse into a loading bay. I had so many questions running around inside my head, but even more of them popped in at that moment.

Is the truck there to pick up or drop off?
Or both?
And either way, what is the cargo?

The shutters came back down. Wes looked at me and said, "There's still time to back out, you know."

I said nothing.

"I mean, until we go in there, we probably won't get into any trouble. Are you sure about this? You're younger than me, you got more to lose."

Part of me wanted to back out now, to just go to the motel and wait until it was time to go to the airport and head back home. This wasn't what I signed up for at the FDA. But I didn't sign up for the FDA; the Resistance signed me up to do their work for them. I felt a strange combination of the need to prove myself and extreme curiosity based on what I had seen here in Lincoln, New Mexico, that made my stomach feel like it was spinning in a blender on its fastest setting.

"No," I said. "I've come this far. I need to know what's going on in there."

"Fair enough. Let's do this."

Wes led the way with confidence in his stride as we reached the end of the path and crossed the empty parking lot towards a door that had been left ajar. He peeked through the gap and scanned the insides as much as he could.

"Looks clear," he said, then placed a finger on the door and very carefully pushed it open. It emitted a long, horror movie creak, but there was no monster behind it waiting to pounce. A long corridor, brightly illuminated by overhead strip lights, stretched out towards another door in the distance.

Wes stepped inside. I followed and closed the door behind us. I'd never felt so out of my depth in my life as we made our way along the corridor.

What was I thinking coming here? I thought. *What good did I think was going to come from this little adventure? Best case? We get discovered, arrested, and prosecuted for trespassing, I lose my job at the FDA, and the Resistance disavow me. Worst case? I guess it depends on what's behind the next door.*

The door at the end of the corridor looked heavy duty. It was solid metal and there was a security card reader in the wall. Tonight, this door had also been left ajar.

"Isn't this a bit easy?" I said.

"What do you mean?"

"These doors have been left open."

"Just lucky, I guess."

"It feels like it should have been harder to get in here. If there really are dirty secrets in here, wouldn't they pay a bit more attention to security?"

"No point worrying about that," Wes said. "We're here now."

He edged the door open to reveal another corridor. Just like the last one, it was empty. We crept along to the end, where it made a turn to the right. Wes peered round the corner.

"Must be the loading bay," he said. "The truck's here."

He took a moment to scan the surroundings. "No one around, though."

I looked round the corner to see what Wes could see. The truck we had seen driving up here was sitting with its rear doors open, backed up against a ramp that led up to thick metal shutters that had been closed.

We stopped at the opening to the loading bay, looking and listening for any indication that we might not be alone. The silence and stillness gave us confidence to run across the loading bay to the truck. Then we edged our way round it to the rear doors, Wes on the right and me on the left. At the same time, we quickly stuck our heads round the edge of the doors to look inside the open cabin in the back of the truck.

"It's empty," he said.

I walked up the ramp to the heavy door. "I guess whatever was in there was unloaded here and taken in there."

Wes sniffed the air. His face contorted into an expression of disgust. "That's one hell of a stink!"

It hit me, too. I walked down the ramp to the truck and found it got stronger.

"What is it?" I said.

Wes smirked. "You ain't been round enough roughnecks in your time, lady. That's the smell of men who ain't washed in a long time. That truck was full of people. My bet is they were hobos."

I felt the word "hobo" trigger me with its political incorrectness, but now was not the right time to call Wes out on it.

"That makes no sense," I said.

"You seen anything in your time here that does, lady?"

I looked at the stinking, empty truck and the ramp leading up to a locked door.

"So what do we do now?" I said.

As soon as the words left my mouth, a loud metallic clunk made me jump, and the shutters began to open.

Chapter 24

We stared into the darkness beyond the open door.

"I guess we go that way," Wes said.

Nothing about this situation felt good, but even with the prospect of walking into a black hole, my curiosity wouldn't let it lie. Every logical fibre in my being told me to turn and run. Then the illogical part of my brain began to speak to me.

It would be such a shame for you to come this far and not discover the truth.

"Come on, then," I said to Wes, taking my first step into the darkness ahead. "It's the only way we're going to find out what's going on up here."

Wes followed me. The raised metal mesh floor rattled under our feet as we made our way into the darkness. I felt certain Wes was waiting for me to say we had made a mistake, and that we should get out of here. I was waiting for him to do the same, but neither of us did. I stopped and turned to look back at the way we had come, yearning for the open, illuminated space of the loading bay. The empty truck looked back at me. Then it disappeared as the metal door slammed shut.

"Oh shit," Wes said under his breath.

Plunged into total darkness, I held out my arms and felt my hand meet Wes'. We held hands, both gripping as tightly as we could.

"So what the hell do we do now?" he said.

I got my phone out of my pocket and turned on the flashlight. It wasn't powerful enough to give us any bearings on our surroundings, but pointing it at the ground allowed us to see our next few steps.

"Better than nothing," I said. "Let's find a way out of here."

"Good idea," Wes said. "And we'd better make it quick, before your battery runs out."

His words gave me a fresh shot of fear, making it a real possibility that we would be scratching around in the dark all night searching for a way out of here.

"Urgh, what the hell is that?" Wes exclaimed.

"What is it?" I said.

"I trod in something."

I shone my phone light at Wes as he examined the sole of his shoe.

"That looks like—"

I couldn't finish my sentence. The realisation hit Wes at the same time. He put his foot down and I raised my phone light, shining it all around us. Pieces of flesh and torn clothing had been scattered in every direction.

"I think we just found out what happened to the homeless guys," Wes said.

"Good evening, Polly."

The voice came from above, freezing us to the spot. Without thinking, I turned off the flashlight, which was met with laughter.

"Hit the lights," the voice said. This time, the voice was familiar.

A second later, our surroundings opened up to us in a low red glow. We were standing in the middle of a large cube-shaped room, with bare concrete walls and a metal mesh floor that was scattered with pieces of homeless guys that glistened in the red light. A walkway ran around the sides of the room, twelve feet or more above us. Directly ahead, two men stood on the walkway, looking down on us. One of them was Jason, the one whose voice I had recognised. The other was Bill, who had a twisted expression on his face that was a mix of disappointment, anger, and I-knew-it smugness.

"What's going on here, Bill?" I said.

He laughed. "I could ask you exactly the same thing, Polly."

"You first," I said, trying my best to put up a brave front.

"Okay," Bill shrugged. "I'll start by telling you what I think you already know. I bet the man who brought you here told you that whatever is going on in the filtering room is just window dressing. He may even have shown you a little trick to demonstrate how that part of the production line doesn't actually do anything. Am I right?"

I looked at Wes. He shrugged.

"Right so far," I said.

"And I bet he then told you that the real milk production goes on up here, at the scary building on the hill. Right?"

"I guess."

"So that's why you've come up here in the middle of the night, to find out the truth."

I said nothing. Then Bill said the words that shook the world around me.

"Thank you, Wes."

I looked at Wes again. His head hung in shame and he whispered, "Sorry, lady."

"You brought me here?" I said. "Why?"

Wes said nothing. He just stood next to me, wringing his hands.

"It's not his fault," Jason said. "We made promises to him."

"What kind of promises?"

"We told him there would be certain consequences if he encouraged you to come here, and different consequences if he didn't."

Now Wes spoke. "So now we're here, are you going to tell me what happened to Al?"

"All in good time," Jason said. "I think Polly here has a million questions she wants to ask first."

"What did they promise you?"

"They said they'd tell me exactly what happened to Al. They said they'd let me in on what goes on up here, and they'd guarantee me a job for life. If I didn't try to get you to come here, I was gonna be toast."

I felt my anger with Wes drop ever so slightly. "They didn't give you a choice," I said. "But try not to worry; we'll work out how to get out of here."

"No, lady. Look, I'm sorry, but they said I just had to get you up here and that would be it." My anger rose again as Wes looked up to Bill and Jason. "That's right, yeah? Now she's here, I can go?"

"Stay where you are," Jason said. "This will all be over soon."

"Enough!" I shouted. "Are you going to tell me what the hell's going on here? You've brought me here for a reason. Get to the point."

Jason turned to Bill and smiled. "You were right about her."

Bill shrugged. "Told you. No doubt in my mind from day one."

"No doubt about what?" I said.

Even at this distance and in the low light, I could feel Bill's piercing stare. "No doubt in my mind that you were a member of the Resistance."

"W-what?" I stammered. "What are you talking about?"

"Cut it out," Bill said. "We've been expecting one of you to worm your way in to this operation. We're only surprised it's taken this long. We decided to force this issue; to give our most curious and unhinged worker the opportunity to sneak in here. We knew his disappearance would grab the attention of the Resistance and, if they had anyone on the inside at the FDA, that person would get assigned to the case, even if they were a total newcomer. Like you."

I said nothing. In my entire life, I had never felt so vulnerable, so used. I was a pawn in a game I didn't know was being played.

"Did you set him up as well?" I said to Wes. He shifted awkwardly.

"They didn't tell me nothing," he said. "Just told me they'd look after me and Al wouldn't come to no harm."

"So what now?" I said.

"Now we know you're a member of the Resistance," Bill said, "all we need to do is find out who assigned you to this inspection. I think it's pretty safe for us to assume that person is also a member, much higher up in the organisation than you."

"So if I'm not going to get out of here, at least tell me why this place exists. Why bother producing cockroach milk in the first place, if it *is* even cockroach milk, and why do it in such a secretive way?"

"Oh, it *is* cockroach milk," Jason said. "You see, cockroach milk is a superfood. All the marketing blurb is correct. It really does contain a combination of vitamins and amino acids that is second-to-none. Where we're from, everyone drinks it, but here, we think most people would struggle to accept where it comes from. That's why we have to be so secretive: so we can mass-produce cockroach milk in the quantities we need without Joe Public deciding we need to be shut down just because the origin of this superfood might be a bit icky. Hard times are coming, Polly. People will die. Cockroach milk is essential to the survival of our race."

"What do you mean, *where you're from? Our race?*"

Jason shook his head. "I think we've told you enough already. How about I show you something, and you piece it all together yourself?" He turned and walked away. Bill looked down at me and said, "It didn't have to be like this, Polly. I gave you a chance."

"What are you talking about?"

"Yesterday, just before we left here. I told you that if you went looking for things we weren't here to find, that's where you'd get into trouble. Jason gave you a chance, too; you didn't have to talk to Wes. Now, you're both in trouble."

"What kind of trouble are we in, Bill?"

I saw him stop short of giving me a straight answer. Instead he said, "You'll see. I don't expect you to understand. This situation is much bigger than you can imagine."

With those words, he turned and followed Jason into the shadows, leaving me and Wes standing in the dull red light, feeling like something very bad was about to happen.

"So what happens now?" Wes said.

"I think we're going to find out what happened to your friend."

The room echoed with a loud metallic clunk, which made us both jump. Then we discovered the wall in front of us wasn't a wall; it was a wide metal door that slowly began to rise. Brighter red light from behind the door crept along the floor towards us. Shadows in the red light moved in strange ways. There was something there, trying to get through the gap under the door as it rose. Whatever it was, it was enormous. Its movements made me think of an angry guard dog, but this thing was so much bigger than any dog.

"Holy shit!" Wes shouted.

In that moment, we both registered what this thing was that was trying to get into the room with us. It was a gigantic cockroach. Imagine the feeling you get when you spot a cockroach in a dusty corner of your house or your favourite restaurant. A shiver runs down your spine; the hair stands up on the back of your neck; and you just want to stamp on it. Now multiply that by a thousand. The only difference was that we had no chance of killing this aberration, and neither of us had a doubt that it had murder on its mind.

Chapter 25

"What are we going to do?" Wes whimpered.

"I've got no idea," I said, scanning our surroundings for anything or anywhere that might give us a slim advantage over this beast. The room was nothing more than a cube with a raised walkway around the perimeter. There was no way up there from down here.

The door opened all the way and the giant cockroach scuttled into the room, its legs moving in sequence like they were driven by machinery.

Then it stopped. I knew nothing about the biology of cockroaches, and the red lighting made it difficult to pick out any detail, but I swear it stopped and looked at us, weighing us up and working out its strategy. We had no choice but to stand there, facing down a giant cockroach, its huge frame silhouetted against the red light spilling through the open door behind. Then it hit me.

"We have to get through that door," I whispered to Wes.

"The one it's just come through?"

"It's the only way out of here."

"How the hell are we going to get round it?"

"We have to split up. You go to the right and I'll go to the left. If it's going to attack, it'll only be able to attack one of us. We need to distract it."

"So whichever one of us doesn't get wiped out makes a run for it? That's not much of a plan."

"Stay sharp. It's bigger than us. I bet we can dodge out of its way."

"That's a hell of a bet."

"Let me know if you've got a better plan."

Wes said nothing.

"Let's do this," I said. "It's coming up with its own plan."

I took two steps to my left. Reluctantly, Wes did the same to his right. The cockroach followed my movements, then followed Wes's. Its head moved from left to right and back again, like it was weighing up its options. We both took two more steps away from each other. I examined the gap between the cockroach and the open door. I had to fight the overwhelming urge to make a run for it, knowing the gap would close long before I got near the door.

Wes looked at me and said, "I'm gonna go for it."

"No!"

My voice came across much louder than I expected. The cockroach turned its attention to me. It shifted on all its legs, angling itself towards me. Out of the corner of my eye I saw Wes edging away from me, eager to take advantage of the diversion I had inadvertently created. I took a step back. The cockroach followed suit, edging forward with all six of its legs. Wes moved forward two more steps.

"Don't do it," I said.

Unable to reply without drawing attention his way, Wes looked at me with wide eyes that I took to mean, *I've got a chance here; let me go for it.* That look in his eye told me I had no option; he was going to make a run for it no matter what I said. The question in my mind was, if he made it to the door, would he shut it on me?

Chapter 26

I knew what I had to do: I had to open up the gap between the giant cockroach and the door to give Wes the best chance of making a run for it. I took two more steps back and the giant cockroach followed me. For another minute, I stood there staring this beast down. Its only movement came from its long, thin antennae, which moved left, right, up, down, and in circles. I felt certain that it was getting its bearings on this room and the two of us in it. My heart was pounding in my chest, my legs shaking with fear and adrenaline.

Did it know this? Could it tell I was afraid? Could it tell I was trying to draw it closer, to give Wes a chance? Why didn't it just pounce on me and get it over with? Maybe it didn't want to feed anymore. Maybe it had its fill on all the homeless people it had been served just minutes before we arrived.

Only a few seconds after that entered my mind, I was proven wrong. The cockroach moved towards me with such speed that I felt like I had stepped into the road in front of a speeding truck. I told myself to move, to get the hell out of the way of the monster thundering towards me, but my body froze. Maybe something in my brain was failing to compute the sight of a giant cockroach, or maybe my fear was so all-consuming that my body was beginning to shut down. I lost all ability to do anything other than close my eyes and brace myself for my inevitable fate as a late night snack.

But nothing happened. With my eyes still shut, I felt a surge of heat. I knew the cockroach was there, just inches from my face, but I couldn't bring myself to look. I had no idea what it was doing, whether it was examining me or playing with me. I didn't care. All I could do was stand there and pray. Every second I continued living from this point onward was a blessing.

I heard the clank of Wes' boots on the floor. He had seen the gap he needed and he was going for it. On the sound of his second step, the hulking mass in front of me shifted. The heat on my face moved away.

I opened my eyes and saw Wes edging towards the door with the huge cockroach between us, facing him. But he had stopped moving. Like me, something had made him stop in his tracks. Maybe this thing had a hypnotic power, or maybe it was just the sheer horror of its existence, but he was unable to move, staring in fear at the monster coming towards him. I told myself it was time for action.

"Run!" I screamed.

The cockroach's antennae twitched at my words. Wes snapped out of his trance and became instantly aware of his predicament. He glanced at the open door and ran. The cockroach followed. With no further thought whatsoever, so did I. Wes made it through the opening. He stopped, frantically looking around for somewhere to go. The cockroach was closing at speed.

"Get out of the way!" I shouted.

Without looking, Wes jumped to his left and fell to the ground. The cockroach slammed into the wall behind the spot where he had been standing just a split second before. Wes scrambled backwards on all fours, his eyes wide with terror. He was cornered. The cockroach was righting itself, turning in his direction to launch a final attack. Wes had seconds left to live. I had to do something.

"Hey!" I shouted.

The cockroach stopped. Its antennae twitched, searching for the source of the interruption.

"Yeah, you!" I shouted again, with no idea what I was trying to do, other than buy Wes a few more seconds of life. The cockroach's antennae twitched again.

"Leave him alone!" I shouted.

The cockroach began to turn. The limitations of its movements were becoming clear to me. Regular cockroaches were fast and nimble. This monster was fast from point A to point B, but its massive bulk made it corner like an oil tanker. Its legs stomped the floor in a pattern, spinning its body slowly in my direction. In its shadow, I spotted Wes trying to get to his feet as quietly as possible. Our eyes met and, without a single word between us, we knew we had a plan.

"Come on then!" I shouted. "Come on then! You want to eat me? Come and get it!"

I kept shouting the same thing, over and over again, praying my words would drown out the sound of Wes as he got to his feet and edged towards the doorway the cockroach was straddling. I moved left and right across the room, shouting as I did so. The cockroach followed me, and I hoped my lateral movement would throw off the targeting it was processing in its giant insect brain.

All the while, Wes was inching towards the panel that controlled the mechanism of the huge metal door. He stretched out a hand, hovering over the button to close the door.

"Okay, Wes, hit it!"

He hit the button. The door mechanism above made a loud clunk. The cockroach's antennae darted in Wes's direction, then upwards, then in all directions. It shifted frantically, its panic obvious. Something was happening that it didn't like the sound of. With a metallic shriek, the door began to close from above.

The cockroach turned to face me and, just as it was about to launch itself at me, the falling door made contact with the mid-point of its back, directly between its thorax and abdomen. Its legs gave way first, forcing its body down to the ground. Its legs and antennae squirmed in pain, but the cockroach's body provided the door with little resistance. The sound of its splintering exoskeleton was drowned out by a scream that did not belong to any creature from the natural world. I covered my ears but could not tear my eyes away from the sight of the giant cockroach as the door hacked it in two.

The door slammed shut. The remnants of the front half of the monster settled on the metal floor, accompanied by the sickening sound of its insides pouring out of its open wounds. The antennae twitched one last time, then the giant cockroach was still. The door rose once again, revealing Wes standing behind it.

"I'm sorry, Polly," he said.

I edged through the door, past the stinking remains of the cockroach. "If you can find a way out of here, all will be forgiven," I said.

"This way," he said, pointing to a door in the corner, on the other side of the putrid remains of the beast we had slaughtered.

Chapter 27

The dark, tight corridors turned us left and right, with stairs going up and down in a path so disorienting that we had no clue whether we were heading towards the exit or further into the belly of this labyrinth. I took my phone out of my pocket, typing in the emergency number as we ran.

333-5510.

"Are you calling the police?" Wes panted.

"No," was the only answer I offered as I heard a male voice on the other end.

"How can I assist?"

"I need help," was all I could blurt out.

"Is this Polly Benton?"

"Yes."

"I can see you're in Lincoln, New Mexico. Is that correct?"

"Yes."

"How can I help?"

"I need to get out of here. I don't really know how to explain it. You'll think I'm crazy and hang up."

"Wait," the man on the other end said. "Lincoln, New Mexico. It looks like you're inside a warehouse belonging to Insectalat. Is that correct?"

"Yes. You need to help me get out of here. Please."

"Okay," the man said, seeming to take a breath as he prepared himself for the task ahead. "Stay on the line. I'll be here the whole time to help guide you out. I just need to do something first."

The static on the line felt like I had lost the most important thing in the world to me. Wes and I stopped as we reached a T-junction. We looked up and down the corridor, not knowing whether we should turn left or right down the identical-looking paths.

"What now?" said Wes.

"Just wait here for a second," I said.

"Wait here?" Wes exclaimed. "For what? We need to get the hell out of here!"

"I think the man I'm talking to can help us get out of here."

"Who are you talking to?"

"Honestly? I've no idea. But I don't think that matters right now."

The voice came back on the line.

"Polly, are you still there?"

"Yes!" I said, the relief obvious in my voice.

"Good. I'm sorry I had to disappear for a moment. An extraction team is on its way to you right now. I need to guide you out of the building. I've got schematics for it. I'm not sure how up to date they are, but I'm not going anywhere until you're safe. Okay?"

"Okay," I said, feeling a boost of confidence at his words.

"First of all, are you alone?"

"No. Two of us."

"Who is the other person?"

"Someone who works on the production line in the factory."

"Okay, let's get you out of there. I can't see exactly where you are in the building, though. Do you know where you are?"

"We're standing at a T-junction. We came in through the loading bay, into a square room, then went through a bunch of twists and turns, and now we're lost."

"That's fine. I think I've worked out where you are. Turning right gives you the shortest path to an exit, but—"

"No 'buts'," I said. "We're moving." I turned right and ran down the corridor, holding my phone to my ear, with Wes close behind.

"There's a door at the end of the corridor," the man said.

He was right. We stopped and I asked him what was behind it.

"This is the biggest room in the whole building. It's safe to say that whatever's behind that door is the reason that building exists."

My heart sank. Everything I had learned so far pointed to this building being the original source of the cockroach milk that was being bottled and shipped from the bogus factory down the hill. When I opened the door, I knew I would find the answers I had been seeking since we got here. But now I didn't care; I just wanted to get us out of here.

"And the exit is in there somewhere?"

"Correct. When you go through the door, you'll be on a raised platform. There are several sets of stairs dotted around the room. Each one has an emergency exit at the bottom. Find your nearest one and make a run for it."

"And pray no one has locked the doors," I said under my breath.

"Good luck," the man said. "Remember, I'm here and I'm tracking the extraction team. They're close. Get out of the building and they'll keep you safe."

"Thanks for your help," I said.

"Not a problem. That's what I'm here for. Might be best if you put your phone away now. I'll be monitoring as much as I can from here."

"Okay," I said. "Wait, what's your name? If I get out of here, I'm going to buy you a drink."

The man on the line laughed. "Sure thing. My name is Adrien Pelsmaekers."

"Thanks for your help, Adrien."

"I'm going to hang up now. You get out of there in one piece."

He hung up. I looked at Wes.

"So what do we do now?" he said.

"Follow me," I said.

I turned the handle and pushed the door open. What was waiting for us on the other side of the door shook us both to the core.

"Holy shit," Wes exclaimed. "They're never gonna let us get out of here."

Chapter 28

We took slow, tentative steps forward onto the raised walkway, our mouths wide open in shock as we surveyed the scene below us, bathed in the same low red light as the room where Bill and Jason had expected us to die. There was no doubt in my mind: *this* was the real factory floor.

I estimated the floor space to be at least double that of the bottling room in the other building. It had been separated into individual glass cubes, with narrow corridors snaking around them. I quickly calculated at least two hundred glass cubes and each one contained a giant cockroach like the one we had met just a few minutes ago. We had the option to walk left or right, heading either way around the rectangular walkway that stretched the full length and width of this enormous space. At each corner of the rectangle, a long, thin ladder led down to the floor. A short walk from the bottom of each ladder, I spotted the green glow of an emergency exit sign. I pointed to the closest exit.

"You're not saying we're going down there?" Wes protested.

"That's the only way we're getting out of here," I said.

Wes sighed. "I guess now is not the time to tell you I'm scared of heights. *And* bugs."

"That's right," I said. "Now is *not* the time."

I took the lead along the narrow walkway. Wes stared directly ahead, but I couldn't help myself from looking down, mesmerised by the sight of the giant cockroaches scuttling around inside their glass cages far below. At that distance, they looked the same as they would have if they were regular size, scuttling around my feet. But as we reached the ladder, I knew they would get bigger and bigger as we descended.

"Do you want to go first?" I asked. I should have looked at Wes first before asking; his face had turned white. "It's okay," I said before he could answer, "let me go first."

I took a deep breath and stepped onto the ladder. It had looked stable enough as we approached, but now that it was taking my full weight, I felt it rattle from side to side in response to my nervous energy.

"Is it safe?" Wes asked, his desperate voice seeking any possible reassurance.

"Safer than staying here," I said. "Come on. The quicker we move, the quicker we get out of here. If the man on the phone was right, someone will be waiting for us on the other side of that emergency exit, ready to take us far away from here. All we need to do is get ourselves down this ladder. We can do this."

"Okay," Wes said. He exhaled and stood an inch taller as he steeled himself.

I led the way down the ladder, trying my hardest to ignore the shaking and rattling, telling myself that with every hand and foothold we were inching closer to safety. As we progressed, I couldn't help myself from taking in the morbid sight of the giant cockroaches. I saw that each cockroach had wires and pipes attached to it, the largest of which appeared to be a thick plastic tube. In some of the glass cages, the tube appeared see-through, but in others it was light blue. Each plastic tube was hooked up to a machine built into the cage, where its contents disappeared into the floor.

"Holy shit!" Wes exclaimed from above. "They're milking them like cattle."

We reached the bottom of the ladder and felt the welcome relief of solid ground under our feet. On all sides, we were faced with giant cockroaches. Some were being milked, and some were scuttling around as much as they could in their glass cages, but all of them looked like they wanted to eat us alive. I turned in the direction of the emergency exit sign, a bright green beacon of hope in the dull red light of this monsters' lair.

The moment we took our first steps, a loud metallic clunk echoed out. It was followed by another, and another. We looked all around, trying to work out what was making the noise. Whatever it was, it wasn't something we wanted to hang around to find out about. We focused on the emergency exit door and ran for it, but after only a few steps a glass door flew open, blocking our path. The cockroach inside that cage wrestled itself free from its milking tubes and made its way out.

"We're dead," Wes said.

"No, not yet," I said, turning away from the giant cockroach that wanted to eat us alive. "Run!"

Chapter 29

We held hands and ran.

The memory of that moment is nothing more than a blur to me now. Flashes of it return to me from time to time, sometimes in dreams, like single still frames from the most terrifying horror movie you've ever seen.

Putting it all together is like trying to complete a jigsaw puzzle with only half the pieces, and you may say, "Polly, it was only a minute out of your life, maybe less, so why can't you remember the whole thing?" My answer would be a recommendation to get yourself chased through a glass maze filled with giant cockroaches that were trying to eat you, then come back to me and compare notes.

What I do know is that we ran; that is my overriding memory, the one feeling from that moment. We had no choice but to run, so we ran. We turned left and right, with nothing guiding our decisions other than instinct and a sheer determination to stay alive. The still images that pop into my mind when I'm least expecting it are the faces—if that's what you can call them—of the giant cockroaches, screaming or snapping at us as we darted out of their way. I can't put these images into any kind of order; all I know is that period of time is nothing more than a terrible mental sludge of terror and confusion that I can't wash away, right up to the point where a lucky, random turn to the left brought us to an emergency exit door. From that moment, my memory turns back from single frames into full motion video.

Our hands reached for the bar across the door, and pushed it, praying that it hadn't been locked. The door burst open, and the swirling, freezing night air outside had never felt so welcoming. That was the first thing that hit us; the second was a dazzling white light in our eyes, and the third was the loud thud-thud-thud of rotor blades belonging to two fully-loaded attack helicopters hovering at the edge of the parking lot. An even louder voice rang out above the din from the lead helicopter's loudspeaker.

"Get out of the way!"

Wes ran to the left and I went to the right. As I turned, I realised that, had we taken a second longer, the first giant cockroach on our tails would have pounced on us.

Instead, I saw its head and body shatter into a cloud of shell fragments and gore. Lines of white-hot bullets lit up the dark night between the helicopters and the stampede of cockroaches trying to get out of the factory's emergency exit. Still, the cockroaches came, and still, the helicopters hovered low over the factory grounds, unleashing a never-ending onslaught of artillery on these monsters, sending them straight back to hell.

Then the volley of gunfire stopped. The narrow emergency exit had become a larger hole in the wall, the brickwork perforated by the gunfire. A cloud of dust and vapour hung in the air, poisoning my airways with its acrid stench. I detected no movement within the scene of destruction.

"Jump in," came the voice from above. "Let's get you out of here."

We got to our feet and stumbled to the helicopters, which the pilots were lowering far enough for us to climb on board. A man sitting behind the biggest gun I had ever seen extended a hand and helped to pull me inside. Out of the corner of my eye I saw Wes clambering into the second helicopter.

"Welcome aboard," the man said, shouting to make himself heard over the din of the rotor blades. "Let's get you strapped in."

I sat down and he secured my seatbelt, then the pilot turned to look at me and I heard his voice over the speaker system

"Good to have you here, ma'am. Are you okay?"

I raised a hand and gave him a thumbs-up.

"That's great. Now, we've just got one more thing to do before we get you out of here."

"What's that?" I asked, but he had already turned his attention back to the helicopter's controls by the time I spoke.

The helicopter banked to the left, then straightened up with its nose tilted downwards, pointing at the factory below. The other helicopter did the same.

"In position," the pilot said over the radio. "Ready? Over."

"Copy that," came the reply from the pilot of the other helicopter. "Ready. Over."

"Fire at will."

A loud whooshing sound was accompanied by the sight of jet trails leaving the underside of the helicopters, heading towards the factory.

The building below erupted in an enormous white fireball. With each rocket that struck its target, the explosion grew even larger. The helicopter shook, its frame shrieking under the stress of each blast wave. I held on tight as I was thrown around in my seat with my eyes fixed on the explosion. I wanted to be absolutely certain there was no chance of anything surviving the attack.

"Primary target neutralised. Confirm: proceed to secondary target? Over."

"Negative. Mission update from home base: leave the other building standing. Over."

"Copy that. Let's get these good folks to safety."

The helicopters banked away from the burning wreckage and headed into the darkness.

Chapter 30

The helicopter touched down in the empty parking lot of an abandoned factory. At first, I thought we were back at the factory in D.C. where I had been introduced to the Resistance; then I remembered we were in New Mexico. Even so, the surroundings were almost identical: a desolate industrial park, with each vacant spot surrounded by tattered, rusting chain link fences.

The pilot shut the engine down and the man who had pulled me aboard escorted me out of the cabin. I saw the other helicopter above us, disappearing into the distance.

"This stop's just for me, right?" I asked him.

"Affirmative," he said, then turned towards the abandoned factory. "This way, ma'am."

I followed him to the front door, which just managed to stay on its rusty hinges as we made our way inside.

I felt like I was in Groundhog Day. He led me through the entrance and into an office that had seen far better days, where he fired up a computer and ran out of the room as soon as he initiated a video call. I stood to attention, waiting for the call to be answered.

The call connected and Jonathan Bigelow appeared on the screen.

"Polly, I'm so glad to see you," he said. "When I heard what was happening, I feared the worst. I can't tell you how relieved I was when I heard our men had picked you up."

"Well, that makes two of us," I said. "Thank you for the rescue."

"It's all part of the job when you're a member of the Resistance. You never know, one day you might find yourself on a rescue mission."

"I'm just glad I lived to tell the tale."

"Very good, Polly. So, now that you are alive, I'd like to ask you to tell me the tale. What happened at the factory?"

"It was my first assignment for the FDA. One of the workers went missing, and I was given the job, along with my partner Bill, who was in on it. He knew that Insectalat were mass-producing their milk using giant, mutant cockroaches, and I bet he knew that if he took along a partner he suspected to be a member of the Resistance—me—then that suspicion would be confirmed if I started snooping around where I wasn't supposed to." I looked at the screen and saw Bigelow nodding along with me.

"You knew about this, didn't you?" I said.

"What do you mean?"

"You knew that place was using those monsters to mass-produce cockroach milk."

"We had strong suspicions, but we'd never managed to get anyone on the inside to make a visual confirmation."

"How many?"

"How many what?"

"How many others like me have gone in there and not made it out again?"

Bigelow paused for thought, then said, "That's not important."

"Who set me up? Of all the assignments I could have been given at the FDA, who made the decision to give me that one?"

"Another member of the Resistance, who now—like you—is being removed from society and is being given a new assignment in an underground role."

"What do you mean, like me?"

"Polly, I'm sorry to say that your short time operating out in the open for the Resistance must come to an end."

"What? Why?"

"You've been exposed. There are people out there who know who you are. They know for certain that you've been working for us. The only thing we can do now is to bring you into our underground operation. Don't worry, you'll be safe. We take good care of all of our members."

"But my mother. What about her?"

"We will do everything we can to make sure she is kept safe."

"Won't the people who own that factory you just blew up try to get to me through her?"

"Maybe, but it's unlikely. Such methods are very old-fashioned. There's no value in them doing anything to your mother. Once they work out that you've survived, they'll know we've decided to keep you out of harm's way."

"Who's *they*, exactly?"

"All in good time, Polly," he said. "The chopper will bring you in to one of our secure facilities, and I'll make sure you get the full debrief. Do you have any other questions?"

"Yes, I do. Where the hell did those giant cockroaches come from?"

Bigelow gave me a wide, conspiratorial grin. "That is a whole story in itself, and one I can't discuss over a public video call, no matter how well-encrypted this channel may be. All will be revealed after we bring you in. You'll need to be sitting down for it, though. Finding out the truth—the *real* truth—about the world is like getting hit in the mouth."

Epilogue

Chapter 31

"Good morning from all of us at CNN. I'm Julia Cabrera, and the time is six a.m. here in New York. Breaking news this morning in the small town of Lincoln, New Mexico, at a factory fire where there were reports of explosions in the early hours. We go now to our reporter on the scene, Gravel Foden. Gravel, what are you learning?"

"Thank you, Julia. I'm here in Lincoln, New Mexico, at the factory belonging to Insectalat. As you can see behind me, the fire crews are still fighting to keep this blaze under control. They were called just after one a.m., with some callers reporting multiple explosions from inside."

"Did you say the factory belongs to Insectalat, where one of the workers went missing earlier this week?"

"That's right, Julia. This is the company that came to prominence in recent months as they became the first corporation to begin mass-producing cockroach milk."

"Now, I have some experience in that matter. I have tried their cockroach milk."

"Really? What did you think?"

"Well, believe it or not, I thought it was fantastic. I was wary about it at first, I have to admit, but when I tried it, I felt like I was full of energy for the whole day. I really started to believe it might be the superfood of the future, like the commercials say."

"Well, it's safe to say that Insectalat's competitors aren't shedding any tears this morning. Local authorities say it's too early to say whether this incident was corporate sabotage or a terrorist attack."

Chapter 32

"We know it wasn't a terrorist attack," Vice President John O'Grady said.

He hit the button on the remote to turn off the TV in the Oval Office. President Frank Oates sat behind his desk with a grave look on his face.

"We'll bury this, Mr. President," O'Grady said.

"I know," Oates said. "That's not what concerns me."

The President got up from his desk and paced over to the window, staring at the dawn light breaking over Washington, D.C.

"We made a mistake when we let Bigelow go, didn't we?"

O'Grady said nothing. He knew this wasn't really a question; it was a statement.

"We all congratulated ourselves on a job well done for the Great American Shoe Throwing. We left Bigelow to finish himself off and, for a while, we thought he had done just that."

"You're convinced he's behind this?"

Oates turned his eyes on his Vice President. "There is no doubt in my mind. He's not the mastermind behind all this—he doesn't have enough money to fund an insurgency on this scale—but he's directing operations like this one."

"And the fake news network we broke down in Macedonia?"

The President nodded.

"We should step up security for your inauguration," O'Grady said, but Oates waved away the suggestion.

"Not necessary," he said. "They won't get what they want by killing me."

"True," O'Grady said, nodding in agreement. "What action do you want to take, Mr. President?"

Oates paced across the carpet of the Oval Office. He didn't tell O'Grady to stand, but the Vice President felt it was the right thing to do.

"Do we know anything about the person who got into the factory?"

"Everything, Mr. President. As a matter of fact, I've met her."

A flash of genuine surprise crossed the President's face. "Really?"

"Her name is Polly Benton. She worked for Synergy Services when we did the deal that helped your predecessor make the decision to go to war. It's a small world."

"Too small," Oates said with a wry smile.

"If we wanted to, could we get to her?"

"Her mother is the key. She's in an institution with a degenerative brain condition."

"Another ex-smoker?"

"Yes, Mr. President."

Oates nodded. "This situation is contained. If she survived, they'll take her underground, but she won't be able to stop worrying about her mother. Sooner or later, she'll make contact, and that'll be our way in. In the meantime, I'll see what my man on the inside can find out."

O'Grady was taken aback at the President's words. "You have a man on the inside, Mr. President?"

"You're not the only one with contacts, John. That's how I know Bigelow has come back from the dead."

"Very good, Mr. President. Now, the Super Bowl is only a couple of weeks away. Does anything that happened in New Mexico affect our plans?"

President Oates stared into O'Grady's eyes, and blinked. Then he blinked again in a different way.

"Nothing has changed, John. The Red Cell operation must proceed. All our plans depend on it."